UNDER GROUND

A STRONG CURRENT TRILOGY BOOK 2

UNDER GROUND

A STRONG CURRENT TRILOGY BOOK 2

GREG OLMSTED

Library of Congress Control Number: 2015905324

ISBN 978-0-9861089-1-4 (trade paperback)

FIRST EDITION

Printed in The United States of America

Book design by Gwyn Kennedy Snider

"Truth will rise above falsehood as oil above water."
MIGUEL DE CERVANTES

"The only thing necessary for the triumph of evil
is that good men do nothing."
ANONYMOUS

CHAPTER ONE

AT FIVE MINUTES BEFORE NINE in the morning, Keahi stood in front of the Head of Department's office, apprehensive and wary, and expecting the worst. In his right hand he had a cup of chocolate macadamia coffee. In his left, he held a brown case file, a rolled-up map, and a white tablet. He set down his coffee mug on a plant stand, adjusted his dress belt and tan Dockers, and smoothed his rumpled, untucked aloha shirt.

He had drunk a lot of beer last night after taking his nephew Liko to the airport for his flight back to Nevada, and he'd worried that he would be dehydrated. But he had also guzzled two large glasses of water and had eaten two apple bananas just before going to bed. That usually helped. He had also taken six aspirins: three before going to bed, three after waking up.

His remedy seemed to have worked, except for a slight pounding in his left temple, which he attributed to his present situation. He picked up his mug and sipped the chocolate coffee.

He had been summoned to discuss the explosion and he was unhappy about that; he didn't want to answer naïve questions, circumnavigate half-baked suggestions, and pretend to appreciate technically unsound advice. It was his belief that technical competency disappeared as one moved up the chain of command, and the Head of Department was at the top.

The door opened and out shuffled Santos, whose hippo-like body came to a stop directly in front of Keahi.

Their eyes met and Santos gave Keahi a penetrating, surprised look that asked, "What the hell are you doing here?"

Keahi responded as if the question had actually been asked. "He wants to talk about the explosion."

"I didn't know you were invited," Santos quipped, his wide mouth expressing displeasure. "I've got to feed the meter. Remember, you're just a responder." He brushed past Keahi and hurried to the elevator, afraid of a traffic ticket.

What an arandapsis, Keahi thought. He couldn't remember what his colleague Toi said it was, but the sound "*arandapsis*" seemed to describe Santos, especially when Santos lost his breath and started wheezing, which he was prone to do. *Yeah, he's an arandapsis.*

Keahi took a deep breath, stepped up to the door and peered inside. The Head of Department was seated at a round table, his long-nose poking at a newspaper as if he were nearsighted. He was slightly built, had short white hair, and sported a well-trimmed, salt and pepper beard. Rumors had already circulated that he was haole – Caucasian – but Keahi had not expected an old man.

On the wall behind him hung a painting of a masted

ship swarmed by a mob of Indians brandishing axes and smashing crates. At first Keahi thought the picture was Captain Cook being hacked to death, and then he guessed it was a warship in Honolulu Harbor in the late nineteenth century, but then he realized it was the Boston Tea Party. He wasn't sure if he liked the painting because it wasn't local history, which made it seem out of place in the Head of Department's office.

He had heard the gossip that the Head of Department was an outsider from Atlanta. How had an outsider, especially a mainland haole, broken through the glass ceiling?

The new Head of Department looked up and said in a pleasant tone, "I'm Jack. You must be Keahi."

Jack stood up and they shook hands. His handshake was firm, strong, and memorable.

Keahi noticed that his clothes were new: a tasteful aloha shirt tucked into a pair of khaki dress trousers, black leather belt with shiny brass buckle, and black leather shoes—the usual dress code for upper management in Hawaii.

"How are you? Have a seat."

Keahi wanted to say, "I'm skewered through and through with office pens, and bound hand and foot with red tape," which was a quote from Charles Dickens's *David Copperfield*. Instead he said, "I'm fine," and set his stuff on the table and took a seat.

"And you?"

"I've got a massive headache from driving into the sun." Jack rubbed his temple. "I need better sunglasses."

"You commute from Kapolei?" Keahi guessed. Kapolei was west of Honolulu and a terrible commute.

"Farther out than that."

"Ko'Olina?"

"Farther."

"Waianae?" But Keahi couldn't imagine an old mainland haole living in Waianae.

"No, even farther. I moved into a beach house near Yokohama Bay."

"Wow! That's *way* out."

"Yes, it is. This morning it took me an hour and forty minutes just to drive from the H2 junction to the office."

"Why Yokohama Bay?"

"My mother lived out there. She died a few months ago and I inherited her beach house." Seeing that Keahi was curious, he added, "I returned for her funeral and decided to stay."

"Oh, I'm sorry."

"Thank you. The house is small but comfortable. I'm fixing it up. It needs a lot of work."

"How do you like Hawaii so far?" Keahi sipped his coffee.

"I was born here but I left in '41, right after Pearl Harbor."

Keahi looked more closely at Jack. His scalp was sunburned pink beneath thin white hair. His face displayed the wrinkles of old age and his hands had veins that bulged. *He must be in his late-seventies—an old man.* Keahi knew no one else in the department that old. He wondered why they hired such an old man.

"Let's go to the courtyard," Jack suggested, rubbing his hands together. "It's freezing in here." He shuddered as they left his over-air conditioned office and stepped to the elevator.

"Is anyone helping you with the case?"

"Yes, Kwon Shin in the Air Office."

Keahi pushed the button for the elevator.

"Air? Why Air? That seems unusual."

"No, not really. The explosion has nothing to do with the Air Office of course, but Kwon knows a lot about gases, including explosive gases."

"Well then, let's see if Kwon can join us," Jack suggested. "Air is on the fifth floor, right? On the way to the courtyard? Let's stop by Kwon's cubicle."

"Sure," Keahi said. He thought, *it sounds like he wants to be involved. If he starts making decisions about the case, he'll muddle things, and Santos isn't going to like this.*

The elevator arrived, they got in, and Keahi felt the acute discomfort of standing close to his new boss in a confined space. He could smell the old man's body odor—kind of grassy. But he also smelled Old Spice cologne. *Do women still like Old Spice?* He pushed the button for the fifth floor and stared straight ahead at the elevator door.

"Tell me about Kwon."

"He's bright. He's committed to protecting the environment."

"Really? Protecting the environment?"

"Yes," Keahi said, suddenly feeling a need to promote Kwon.

"Well, we'll see."

Keahi wanted to add, *and Kwon doesn't suffer fools gladly, so don't say anything stupid. He'll never forgot it.* In fact, Keahi thought that Kwon's style was Socratic and confrontational. He suspected that Kwon was unpopular because he was so analytical and took his work so seriously.

They got off on the fifth floor, walked through the Air Unit to Kwon's cubicle, and found him seated at his desk, drinking a cup of coffee. He was wearing a white shirt, black pants and rainbow suspenders. Today he looked like a Mormon trying to make a loud fashion statement. *It could have been worse,* Keahi thought. *He could be wearing his aloha shirt with the bicycle helmet motif.*

On one wall of Kwon's cubicle was a map of the universe showing the stars, galaxies and constellations of the Northern Hemisphere. "You're a stargazer," Jack said in a confident voice, announcing himself and studying the map.

"Yes," Kwon answered. He sat up straight in his chair. His eyes focused on Jack, analyzing him. "I got that poster at the Adler Planetarium."

"In Chicago?" Jack asked.

"Yes, I was attending a conference on hazardous air pollutants."

"You're an astronomy major." It was more a statement than a question.

"Yes, I have my master's from the University of Hawaii."

"I'm Jack, the new Head of Department." Jack held out his hand. "You must be Kwon."

"Yes." Kwon stood up and they shook hands. Keahi saw the relief on Kwon's face as Jack stopped short of squeezing his arthritic hand.

Jack put his finger on the black space between the stars. "I heard that space is mostly just hydrogen, and that we are mostly just water—hydrogen and oxygen. Good old water H_2O. What do you think, Kwon?"

"Well, we are hydrogen—the same hydrogen that formed the stars." Kwon rubbed his chin, choosing his words carefully. "Three-fourths of everything in space is hydrogen. The stars shine because of it."

"Hydrogen makes the stars shine?" Jack asked.

"Yes. The hydrogen in space collects and then tremendous gravitational pressures convert it into helium, which powers the nuclear fusion in the stars, and that makes them shine. Then, as the stars grow older, some go supernova, like the one your finger is near—the Rosette Nebula near the Monoceros region of the Milky Way. Those explosions create oxygen, carbon, nitrogen and all the other elements of the cosmos. And that's what we are—a composite of the basic elements of the cosmos. So, yes, you are right: we are hydrogen and other star stuff."

Keahi could tell that Jack was genuinely interested in Kwon, which he found amazing for someone in management. It was his experience that managers were either too insecure or too full of themselves to have meaningful relationships with their staff.

"What's this?" Jack pointed to Korean calligraphy, framed in a black, eleven-by-seventeen inch frame, hanging above Kwon's desk.

"To the stars through difficulties," Kwon answered. "It's a translation of Latin into Korean. It's from the Latin, '*Per aspera ad astra*.'"

"And this?" Jack pointed to a smaller, framed picture on the corner of Kwon's desk.

"The Kingdom of Choson." Noticing that Jack didn't understand, Kwon added, "My grandparents were from Korea, the Kingdom of Morning Calm."

"It looks beautiful."

"It was at one time," Kwon said.

Jack changed the subject. "I've been following the Freon case."

Kwon shrugged and said nothing, so Jack continued, "I think you did an excellent job laying the foundation for the case. If the federal investigators get a conviction, it will be a result of the original work that you did."

Keahi knew that Kwon had been terribly disappointed when the case had been removed from state jurisdiction and given to the feds. Kwon had initiated the Freon case against the smugglers, yet the feds had told him to back off, to let them pursue it as a criminal investigation. It had been difficult for him to sit back and to watch the feds step in and take over.

"Thanks," Kwon said.

He's beaming, Keahi thought. *Someone finally recognized and acknowledged his work.*

"You're assisting Keahi with the Kehena Kare case?"

Kwon glanced at Keahi.

Keahi raised an eyebrow, acknowledging the glance. He nodded yes with his eyes.

"Yes. I've tried to help."

"Well, we are about to discuss it. Would you like to join us?"

"Sure."

"Good! Very good! Shall we go to the courtyard?"

According to office rumors, the courtyard had become Jack's second office. Keahi now understood why: none of the windows were designed to open and the air conditioning system had overcooled the building. The courtyard, however, was outside and warm. Perfect for someone Jack's age.

Before Jack arrived, the courtyard had been unused, overgrown with weeds, and littered with trash. Everyone knew that he had moved in a large picnic table made out of recycled plastic—supposedly because it fit the department's goal to promote recycling. Staff followed his lead and brought in potted plants: a kumquat tree, a dwarf lime, and fish-tail palms. Soon spices followed, rosemary and basil and mint.

Now the courtyard was a pleasant outdoor work area, and it was often used for meetings. In fact, the courtyard had become so popular that it was signed out weeks in advance.

When they arrived, Jack sat down at his picnic table and Kwon sat down across from him. Keahi chose to sit beside Kwon.

"What happened out there?" Jack asked. Although he didn't specifically mention the playground, Keahi knew that he was talking about the explosion.

"Sir, shouldn't we wait for Santos?" Keahi asked.

"Please, don't call me 'sir.' It makes me feel old. I am old, but I don't want to be reminded of it." He smiled.

Keahi nodded his head and said, "Okay."

"Are you wondering how an old man like me got this job?"

"No," Keahi lied.

"Well, with my age comes considerable experience. I was interviewed by phone while I was packing my things in Atlanta. You see, I was moving back to Hawaii anyway, and had heard about the job and Federal Expressed my application. They offered me the job based on several telephone conversations and my experience and excellent references—and probably because I graduated from Punahou." Punahou was an elite, local, private high school. Its alumni included many notables, including President Barrack Obama in 1979.

You may have been born and raised here, Keahi thought, *but you're still a haole. If you fumble, you'll be sidelined. If you're successful, their jealousy will remove you. Unless you're part of the old boy's network, which I doubt, you'll never be accepted.*

"And no one checked your age?" Kwon blurted out.

Keahi averted his eyes and looked at the kumquat tree. It was filled with ripe brown fruit.

"It's not on the application," Jack replied.

"But they could have estimated it from your years of service," Kwon suggested.

"Perhaps. But I only listed my environmental experience. And I didn't receive my Ph.D. in Environmental Engineering until I was in my late thirties. I didn't list my earlier degrees or my public health experience." He smiled. "I guess they just added up my environmental experience."

Keahi looked at Kwon. He was clearly impressed with Jack.

Keahi looked across the table hard at Jack. *I'll need to protect my job when the spotlight shines on this haole.*

"Anyway, once they offered me the job and I accepted and moved here, it was too late for them to change their decision. I'll tell you, though, they *were* surprised!"

"How about the residency requirement?" Kwon asked.

"It's funny you should ask, because after I started work, personnel did challenge my residency. But I own land here— my mother's beach house. And I immediately registered to vote. When I passed the required physical they gave up and threw in the towel."

"Good for you," Kwon said.

They'll get rid of you, Keahi thought. *They'll find an excuse.*

"So, where were we?" Jack collected his thoughts. "I asked about the explosion. Didn't I?"

When Keahi still hesitated, Jack added, "I already talked to Santos about it, if that's what's bothering you. I talked to him earlier this morning. He'd be here now, but he had to move his car."

Keahi still balked, still unsure about proceeding without Santos.

But before he could object again, Kwon asked Jack, "Did someone complain about the investigation? About how we were handling the investigation?"

"No, I am interested because children were hurt. One child is dead. Another is in guarded condition. I need to know what happened. We need to prevent this from happening again."

That answer encouraged Keahi; consequently, he opened up and explained the case in detail, including his concerns about the former laundry business—now the Kesago Club. He also told Jack about the meeting with the owner of the club, "the Captain," and his consultant, Alegado. Keahi explained that he did not trust consultants. He trusted only documented evidence and what he could observe with his own eyes. He said that the only thing worse than a consultant saying "trust me" was a consultant saying "it's failsafe."

Jack then listened attentively as Kwon explained about the explosive nature of flammable gases.

And then Santos arrived. "Sorry I'm late," he said to Jack, "but I had a hard time finding you. I didn't know where you had gone." Santos grabbed a plastic stool from under a dwarf kumquat tree and moved it to one end of the picnic table.

After he brushed off some leaves, he climbed onto the stool, out of breath. Riding the elevator had winded him.

Keahi noted that Santos was too large to sit at the picnic table, thus he had to sit on the stool. The stool, though, was too small, and Santos's large belly dropped between his knees.

It must be terrible to be in such poor health, Keahi thought.

"Why not investigate the laundry area, that club, what was its name? Kesago?" Jack asked.

"Because it's clean," Santos stated, speaking up. "The site is clean."

"I see," Jack said. "What is your opinion, Kwon?"

Santos interjected, "Kwon doesn't know anything about it. He works in the Air Unit."

"I'd still like to hear his opinion."

The gentle rebuke upset Santos and his face turned red.

Kwon's eyes darted from Jack to Santos's flushed face, and then back to Jack. "First we need to determine if there is a plume of gasoline under the playground," he said.

"And if there is a plume?" Jack asked.

"If there is a plume we need to delineate its horizontal and vertical extent."

"How?"

"Extend our investigation, if necessary, to the neighboring properties, including the former laundry. If there was a release of gasoline we need to find its source and control it."

Santos turned his head away from Jack and looked hard at Kwon, threateningly.

"But how would you do it, Kwon?" Jack asked, ignoring Santos. "If you were to conduct the investigation, how would you do it?"

"I would use a passive soil gas survey, one block in each direction from the explosion. I would also use magnetic and ground-penetrating sonar to look for abandoned tanks and pipelines. And I would install vapor monitoring wells—first in the playground, then on the surrounding properties."

Keahi heard the cooing of a dove.

Jack leaned forward, placed his hands on the table, and looked Kwon in the eyes, then Keahi, and then Santos. "I met with both of the boys' parents," he said. "I promised them that we would do our best to find out what happened. I promised that it would not happen again."

Jack then made his decision: he directed Santos to supervise the expansion of the investigation to include the neighboring properties. And he told Keahi and Kwon that he wanted daily progress reports.

Santos was shocked. His large mouth was agape, his lower molars visible.

And then Jack abruptly changed the subject. "I'm having a department beach party at Bellows Beach Park. It will be barbecue, volleyball and swimming. I expect to see all of you there. Okay?"

Keahi had seen a flyer announcing the party. At that time, like most of the staff, he had resolved not to attend. Why spend his weekend doing something related to work? However, turning down a personal invitation from the Head of Department....

"Yeah, sure," Keahi and Kwon replied in unison. Besides, how could they refuse a guy who had just put Santos in his place?

CHAPTER TWO

KEAHI SPIKED THE VOLLEYBALL for the game point, aiming so as not to hurt anyone. "All right!" Toi yelled and slapped him on the back. "Way to go!"

Playing volleyball in the shade of the ironwood trees at Bellows Beach Park was an enjoyable way to spend a lazy afternoon. Winning the last game was a bonus. Moreover, the weather was perfect for a cookout, and the trades were blowing onshore, across Waimanalo Bay, stirring the long needles in the ironwoods.

"Swim?" Toi asked Keahi.

"No." He knew that Toi wanted to cool off, but first he wanted to say a few words to Jack, who was barbecuing their lunch. "I need an ice-cold soda first."

Jack had impressed Keahi during the meeting in the court-yard. He had asked good questions, and he had listened to Kwon's advice. He remained calm and didn't get pushed into making a bad decision by Santos's bullying. And he had made a bold and assertive decision: the investigation would be expanded to the neighboring properties. His style was certainly different from the passive-aggressive style of the other managers.

Keahi was also impressed with Jack because he had managed to return to Hawaii. Most people who left the islands never returned, except as tourists or to visit family. Jack was unusual.

When Keahi headed for the grill Toi followed him. Everyone else, a dozen hot and sweaty co-workers, headed for the ocean.

Jack had set up his mid-size Smokey Joe and portable table and chairs and blue tarp on the edge of the wide, sandy beach, in a grove of ironwoods. The grove lay between two lazy streams, Waimanalo and Puha. The military maintained the area and opened it to the public on weekends and holidays, so the beach was clean, except for what washed in from neighboring beaches.

"Why aren't you two swimming with everyone else?" Jack asked as Keahi and Toi approached the grill.

"Later," Keahi said. He fished a carbonated passion-or agave drink out of the cooler. Toi found a diet ice tea. "We thought we'd check on the chef first."

The coals were one layer deep and had a light coating of white ash. A chunk of keawe wood lay on top of the coals, smoking.

They watched Jack transfer marinated chicken breasts from a plastic container to the grill, using long-handled tongs. After the chicken seared on both sides, he set the lid on the kettle. Smoke streamed through vent holes in the lid.

Keahi stepped up to the grill and stood in the smoke. He spread his arms wide and inhaled deeply and said, "I love the smell of barbecue."

"Well, you can take it home with you now," Toi said, her voice singing with laughter.

"That's the idea." He returned her smile.

Keahi looked at Jack's yellow T-shirt and tan Bermuda shorts. White curly hair covered his legs and forearms. His clothes and hands were still clean, yet he undoubtedly smelled like charcoal and keawe, too.

They watched Jack remove the cellophane wrapping from a large brisket and set the thick slab of red meat on a white platter on the portable table. Then he shook black pepper profusely from a small red can until the entire surface of the brisket was black. The wind kicked up and blew a puff of pepper in Toi's direction.

"Do you swim?" Jack asked Toi.

"Oh, yes. I love the ocean."

"Her nickname is Little Ama," Keahi said.

Jack smiled. "Little Ama?"

"After the Ama divers of Japan, the ones that dive for pearls."

Toi blushed. Embarrassed to be the center of attention, she burst out with a description of the ocean, which she described as a place of adventure and curiosity and passion.

Jack listened attentively, pausing frequently to make eye contact with Toi as he added a dozen mounds of minced garlic—each the diameter of a nickel, and a half-inch high— across the surface of the brisket. Then he sprinkled on four or five dry spices, filling in the spaces between the mounds of wet garlic. Again the wind picked up and the spices began to blow off the brisket. Keahi stepped back. Jack generously poured lemon juice over the dry spices and diced garlic and massaged everything into a paste with a spoon, and then he smoothed the spices evenly across the top of the brisket. Lemon juice flowed over the sides of the dark red meat and pooled along the perimeter of the white serving platter. Keahi had never seen anything like it before.

"A great tenderizer," Jack said, noticing Keahi's curiosity.

And then Kwon arrived. He marched straight to the grill and demanded, "Is Masako here?"

Jack looked at him, raised an eyebrow, and then continued arranging onion slices on top of the brisket.

Suddenly realizing that he should have said hi to everyone first, Kwon said, "Hi guys." It was clearly an afterthought on his part.

"Glad you could make it," Jack replied, smiling at him.

"Was she here earlier?"

"No," Keahi said. Why was Kwon so interested in Masako? For weeks now, she had been the target of his derogatory, inappropriate comments. And those comments, often racial, had left Keahi feeling very uncomfortable. What was his motivation?

For his part, Keahi liked Masako, though he didn't know much about her. He knew that she had a few casual friends at work, although he wasn't one of them, but he doubted that she had any real friends. That wasn't her fault, necessarily; most locals already had high school friends and extended family. Consequently, they were polite, did their own thing, but they also did lunch without you. At least no one was giving her the go-by yet.

"You missed a good game of volleyball," Jack told Kwon. He removed the lid and leaned it against the side of the grill. Smoke billowed out. He quickly turned the golden-brown chicken with the tongs and rearranged them.

"I can't play," Kwon said.

"Why not?" Jack asked, glancing at Kwon.

"Because of my arthritis."

"It's that bad?" The flames shot up around the glistening pieces of chicken. Jack put the lid back on the grill.

"Oh, yeah! If my wrist bent—let's say I hit the volleyball and it bent my wrist—I'd pass out. I'd drop like a coconut. It would be too embarrassing. But I enjoy watching a good game."

"Rheumatoid arthritis?" Jack adjusted the vent holes until steady streams of smoke billowed out like smoke from the nostrils of a dragon.

"Yeah."

Jack made eye contact with Kwon and nodded.

Keahi listened as Kwon told Jack all about the medications that he took and the side-effects and how frustrating and debilitating the disease was.

When Kwon finally stopped talking about himself, he looked around.

Probably looking for Masako, Keahi thought.

"I think it was terrible that the feds took over your Freon case," Toi told Kwon.

"Well, it's probably for the best," Kwon replied. "The department doesn't take aggressive enforcement anyway." He glanced at Jack to see if his comment was out of line. Jack didn't challenge him.

"Does anyone know if Masako is coming?" Kwon asked.

"You seem awfully interested in her," Keahi said, chiding him.

Kwon shoved his hands into the pockets of his shorts. "I'm going for a walk."

"Don't stay away too long or the chicken will disappear," Keahi warned, smiling. "We're hungry."

Kwon frowned. He walked to the edge of the ironwoods, turned to his left, and took off down the beach towards Waimanalo Stream.

No sooner had he left the group than Masako arrived.

Keahi thought she looked beautiful in her three piece skir-tini: a fashionable—and clearly expensive—swim suit and cover-up.

He introduced Masako to Toi and Jack.

"Whatever you're grilling smells wonderful," Masako said.

"Spice-smothered brisket, and chicken marinated in my secret recipe."

That started a conversation about secret recipes, and gradually Masako opened up, too. First she told Jack about her strong science background and master's degree in chemical engineering, which served her well in her current position in the Hazardous Waste Unit. Jack was interested when she said she'd earned her degree in Japan, so he began asking her questions about Japan. Masako talked about living in Japan after her mother died and her father temporarily abandoned her. She even told him about her second job, dancing at a nightclub.

Keahi was surprised to learn about her dancing, but he was even more surprised that she told Jack about it.

Who tells their boss that they have a second job as a stripper? Jack, however, seemed to take it all in stride without any judgment.

He has a gift for making people feel comfortable, Keahi thought. *People trust him.* Keahi saw it happen in the office with Kwon, who had shared his love for astronomy. Earlier he saw it happen with Toi, as she talked on and on about the ocean. And just now, he saw it happen with Masako, as she shared about living in Japan, her mother's death, and being a stripper.

It seemed to Keahi that once Jack discovered what you were interested in, what you were truly enthusiastic about, or what was important to you, he was determined to possess it, as if he had suddenly unearthed an uncut, precious gem. He behaved like an old prospector who couldn't resist running his hand along a seam of newly discovered gold. Whatever Jack's motivation, he wanted to understand you.

Masako now turned her attention to Keahi. "How is the investigation going?"

"Okay, but slow." Keahi told her about his meeting with Jack, Kwon and Santos in the courtyard. He explained that Jack had approved a scaled-up investigation, including neighboring properties. Then he told her about Santos going to the union with a grievance—something about changing work conditions without negotiating. Pure bullshit. Because the grievance was against Jack, Keahi decided not to discuss it further. Nevertheless, he had heard the rumors. According to the office grapevine, the complaint stated that the use of subsurface sampling tools involved a change in working conditions that required negotiation with the union.

Also listed were thirteen minor complaints against Jack, including one denouncing the use of a public courtyard for work-related meetings. The union was demanding that Jack remove the picnic table and restore the courtyard to its original condition.

"What a dinosaur," Masako said. She glanced at Jack. He was slowly turning the chicken, quietly listening. "The union, not Santos."

He's an arandapsis, Keahi thought. *Which is not much better.*

"Discover anything?" Jack asked Keahi.

"Yes, I think someone did some work at the club. The ground was disturbed. It's very suspicious. But we have no witnesses and no one's talking."

"What kind of work?" Jack asked.

"I think they removed a tank—probably a gasoline tank."

Jack frowned and poked at the brisket on the table with the long-handled tongs.

"Yes," Keahi continued. "They probably had both a heating oil tank and a gasoline tank: a diesel tank to heat hot water for washing laundry, and a gasoline tank to fuel their delivery trucks."

"Did you share your suspicion with Santos?"

"I did, yes. But he still swears there was only a heating oil tank, no gasoline tank."

"So what evidence do we have?"

"Nothing. I talked to the neighbors, but no one saw anything. If there was a tank it has disappeared. So, we are back to looking for a plume of gasoline. We put out a contract for installing five vapor monitoring wells and conducting a passive soil-gas survey, which will include the club."

"You're waiting for a contract?" Masako asked.

"Yeah," Keahi said.

"God, nothing gets done slower than a contract!"

"Yeah, tell me about it," Keahi said. "I feel like I'm riding a turtle."

He glanced at Jack, quickly, for his reaction. Jack appeared preoccupied turning the chicken on the grill, but Keahi knew that he was listening.

Keahi's attitude about Jack's involvement in the investigation had changed. He now welcomed his input. And Masako was correct, there was nothing slower than bureaucracy.

"Jack," Keahi said, "would you like me to watch the grill so you can take a swim?"

"No. I didn't bring my suit. Besides, I enjoy barbecuing."

And talking story, Keahi thought. Actually, he was relieved that Jack had said no; Keahi didn't like messing with another man's grill. He had only made the offer to be polite.

"Masako?" Keahi asked. "Want to join us?"

"Sure, I'd like that."

So he strolled with Masako and Toi through the ironwoods to the beach, and then to the water's edge. Masako removed her pull-on skirt to reveal a black brief printed with large, white cresting waves that could be mistaken for slivers of moon against a black sky. She dropped the skirt onto the sand. Keahi was already wearing board shorts. Toi stripped to a modest two-piece suit.

As they waded into the ocean, Keahi looked back. Jack was alone at the grill, shrouded in smoke.

After their swim, everyone gathered around the grill except for Kwon, who had not returned from his walk. Everyone helped themselves to the barbecued chicken, tender brisket, grilled ahi, macaroni salad, potato chips, and the large platter of fresh grilled vegetables. Keahi grabbed another carbonated fruit drink.

Everyone ate and talked story and were relaxed, and it appeared that the afternoon cookout had been a success, but then Keahi saw Kwon sauntering down the beach. His relaxed mood disappeared as quickly as spilled gasoline evaporates on hot concrete.

And Masako? She saw Kwon too, and she retreated with a plate full of food into the cool shadows of the ironwoods.

Arriving, Kwon said hello to Keahi. Then he carefully surveyed everyone in the barbecue area. He seemed disappointed, which Keahi attributed to his failure to find Masako. Keahi, knowing where to look, could see her silhouette against the sky, partly hidden by broad, twisted tree trunks. She was leaning against an ironwood tree, gazing out at the ocean, eating her plate lunch.

Kwon half-heartedly broadcast a question: "Did you see the historical marker? Just up the beach?"

When no one nibbled, Kwon continued, "A Japanese soldier grounded a midget submarine. Right here, on this reef. He became the first prisoner of war."

A further silence. Everyone was chewing their food.

"The sub was part of a sneak attack."

Keahi glanced from Kwon to Masako and saw her head cock to one side. She could hear him.

"A sneak attack."

Her silhouetted head moved side-to-side.

"Unprovoked."

She stepped out from the ironwood trees. "No! There was no sneak attack!"

Startled, Kwon tilted his plate. A chicken leg rolled off and fell to the sand. Regaining his composure he said, "Then how do you explain the historical marker?"

"The marker has nothing to do with sneak attack. There was no sneak attack."

"You've got to be kidding!"

"No, Japan was defending herself."

"A Japanese mini-sub ran aground here in Hawaii, and you say it was a defensive maneuver? That sub was a long way from Japan, don't you think?"

Someone laughed.

"No," Masako answered, her voice taut and quivering. "The United States embargoed Japan's oil. That started the war. The U.S. cut off Japan's supply of oil. Japan had to defend herself."

"Is that what they taught you? Your teachers in Japan?"

Keahi sighed, upset. He noticed that Toi and Lim were looking at Kwon incredulously. Jack appeared upset, too; he was listening, holding a half-filled plate of food.

Everything went tense.

And then Toi jumped in. "Jack, this is very good. The brisket is tender."

"There was no sneak attack," Masako reiterated. "That's the American perspective." She hesitated for emphasis, or perhaps because she was trying to control her temper. "What I know is this: the Japanese defended themselves from American imperialism."

Jack then entered the furor. "Masako, I can assure you that Japan was the aggressor. I lived through it. I saw the Japanese planes. One flew over my mother's house! And believe me, we did not expect the Imperial Japanese Navy to attack us. Especially on a Sunday morning."

Masako said nothing, her eyes having shifted to Jack.

Jack set down his fork on his half-eaten plate of food, and then continued, "Can I tell you a story about the beginning of the war?"

"Sure," Masako said, nodding respectfully to Jack.

"I lived through it," Jack said. "A week after the attack, I asked my stepfather for permission to join the Marines. You see, most of my classmates enlisted, but I couldn't because I was only seventeen. I was underage. I couldn't enlist unless my stepfather signed a waiver."

"Did he sign it?" Masako asked.

"No. He refused."

"Why?"

Jack cleared his voice. "Because he was Japanese."

Jack waited for the impact of that statement to register before he continued. "I remember very clearly, exactly what he said: 'No. I will not allow you to fight against Japan. We have family and friends in Japan.'

"I remember my mother entered the room while we were arguing. I had never argued with my stepfather, and my mother was shocked.

"She picked up on the argument quickly: I wanted to enlist, my stepfather was opposed." Jack became thoughtful, recalling the events of that afternoon. "She didn't want me to leave home, of course. And she especially didn't want me to go to war. So she took my stepfather's side. My mother told him not to sign the waiver, not to give me his permission.

"We exchanged some heated words and I left home that day. Later, I went to the recruitment office with several class-mates who were old enough to enlist. I had only five months to go until I was 18 years of age, but I didn't wait. I lied about my age and we all joined the Marines."

Masako stood still, respectfully listening.

"Masako, I wanted to enlist because I was angry. And I was angry because it was a sneak attack."

"Masako," Lim said, getting her attention. "Only a few hours after they bombed Pearl Harbor, they bombed the Philippines, too. And they were not expecting an attack either. And several days later they invaded," Lim continued. "The Filipinos resisted, but the Japanese captured Manila."

"And they slaughtered a million Filipinos!" Kwon added.

"I don't know about that," Keahi said, trying to defuse some of the tension. He got up, went over to the table, and started opening the dessert dishes. "But I do want dessert. Anyone else?" He started cutting a chocolate sheet cake. "Surely someone besides me wants a piece of chocolate cake?"

"When the United States won the war," Masako said, ignoring Keahi, "they rewrote history according to their own perspective. The true victims of the war—the women and children—they were in Nagasaki and Hiroshima. *They* are the innocent victims."

Keahi knew that Kwon wouldn't let that pass. And he didn't. "The Japanese killed more women and children in China than died in Nagasaki and Hiroshima!"

Keahi sighed.

Masako stood still, her arms crossed in front of her, tightly against her chest. There was no mistaking that body language: she considered the discussion over.

Kwon thought otherwise. "Did your teachers tell you about the Rape of Nanking?"

Masako didn't answer.

Keahi started passing out pieces of chocolate haupia cake.

"Where is Nanking?" Toi asked, jumping in with a question.

"In the center of eastern China," Lim answered. "It's the capital of Kiangsu Province. Nanking is on the Yangtze River."

"Is it close to where you were born?" Toi asked Lim.

"No," Lim replied. "I was born many miles from Nanking."

"In a large city or in the—"

"Masako," Kwon broke in, "do you know what happened in Nanking?"

Masako stared at him, her eyes full of disbelief, her arms still crossed in front of her. Again, she didn't answer.

Silence filled the barbecue area.

Keahi took the break in the argument to shove a piece of cake and a fork into Kwon's hands. "Hey, let's talk about something else, okay?"

Kwon ignored him. "Lim, you should tell her about Nanking."

"I thought everybody knew about the Rape of Nanking," Lim replied. He looked around and was surprised by everyone's blank expression. "Why don't you tell them about it, Kwon?"

"Because you are Chinese, not me," Kwon answered.

Lim studied Kwon for a moment. "That makes no difference," he said.

Keahi wished that the trades could carry the stink away. "I'm going for a stroll." His voice cracked and he had to clear his throat. "Would anyone like to join me? Toi? Masako?"

They both nodded yes.

"Kwon?" Jack asked.

"What?"

"I could use your help with the grill." Jack's voice was calm, yet assertive. "Do you mind?"

"Um," Kwon hesitated. He clearly wanted to continue his pursuit of Masako, but Jack was the boss.

And it wasn't necessary for Jack to speak again; he just waited for Kwon to make eye contact, and then it was over. Jack was the boss, Kwon, the subordinate.

"Sure," Kwon replied. But his frown, which he was unable to control, exposed his true feelings. He clearly wanted to continue his interrogation of Masako.

Thank God! Keahi thought.

Both Masako and Toi joined Keahi for a stroll up the wide beach to Puha Stream. Keahi chose to go towards Puha Stream because he didn't want to see Santos, who was down at the other end of the beach. Santos had stopped by the picnic earlier—just long enough to say hi and to tell everyone that he was going fishing at the mouth of the Waimanalo Stream. Keahi wanted to avoid meeting him.

Keahi was the closest to the ocean, then Masako, and then Toi. As they walked along, small, gentle waves broke against the shore and crawled up the beach to within inches of his feet. They kept their slippers on because the sand was dirty with brightly colored bits of weathered plastic and glass.

"That conversation went down the toilet fast," Toi said, trying to lighten the tension they still felt.

"I don't know what has gotten into him," Keahi said. Kwon had often been insensitive, never quite understanding what other people wanted or needed. He wasn't very social. He was usually quiet, doing his work silently and by himself. Keahi had never known him to be rude and mean. "I don't know why he is attacking you."

"He doesn't like me," Masako said. "I don't know why either. I've never done anything to him." Her eyes began to water. "Why is he so hateful?"

Keahi sullenly kicked a piece of a plastic cup that had washed ashore. "Look at this."

"It will be here for hundreds of years," Toi said, trying to keep the tears from her eyes, too. "The waves will keep grinding it and grinding it, finer and finer, until you'll need a microscope to see it, but the plastic will still be here, still mixed in with the sand. For generations."

Yeah, the jagged and sharp edges are being ground away, Keahi thought, *but it's still plastic. Still glass.*

They continued walking down the beach, each of them quiet and lost in their own thoughts, until they came to Puha Stream, where they turned around.

As they started back, Keahi said to Masako, "I'll talk to him. See if I can figure out what his problem is."

They stepped into each other's footprints.

Masako turned to Keahi, "When you talk to him, I want you to tell him something for me." Tears had formed in her eyes.

"Okay," Keahi said.

"Tell him that if he harasses me like that again, I will file a grievance." A tear slid down her cheek. "I'll file a complaint with the Hawaii Civil Rights Commission!"

"I'll tell him," Keahi said, his voice sad.

Keahi's cell phone rang and he took the call. While he talked, Masako and Toi took turns throwing chunks of dead, sun-bleached coral back into the ocean.

When he closed his cell phone Toi asked, "What's up?"

"There was another explosion near the playground."

"Was anyone hurt?" Toi asked.

"The caller had no details. I need to tell Jack and then drive out there."

"I'm staying here," Masako said, wiping the tears from her eyes. "I'm not going back to the picnic."

"I don't want to go back either," Toi said. "I'll stay with you, Masako."

"Thanks."

They told Keahi to be careful, then they cleared debris from a small area of sand and sat down.

When Keahi had gotten a ways down the beach, he glanced back. They were still sitting together, facing the ocean, and Toi had put her arm around Masako's shoulders.

He turned and quickened his pace. When he got back to the picnic area, he told Jack about the call and the explosion.

Kwon volunteered to tag along, as Keahi hoped he would. Jack gave his approval: "Be careful and keep me posted."

"I will," Keahi nodded.

CHAPTER THREE

As Keahi and Kwon drove down Hughes Road past the Air Force guard post, Keahi calculated the quickest route from the windward shore to the child care center: Kalanianaole Hwy to the Pali Hwy to Hwy 1 to Kehena. It would take them at least fifty minutes, maybe forty minutes if the traffic was good.

Unfortunately, they found themselves behind a pickup truck, meandering along the windward coast. The ocean was on their right, hidden by brush and non-native trees and dilapidated houses. The towering Koolau Mountains were on their left—sheer cliffs with sharp, vertical ridges that looked chiseled. It was impossible to pass safely; there were too many curves.

Keahi took three deep breaths, holding each breath for a moment, then exhaling slowly. Pete, his former partner, had shared this simple technique for reducing anxiety. Keahi relaxed his grip on the steering wheel and allowed himself to settle back into his seat.

He turned on the radio and channel surfed, trying to find news about the explosion. He settled on FM 105.1, a Hawaiian music station, hoping to catch a news report.

He looked over at Kwon. "What's going on between you and Masako?"

"Between Masako and me?"

"Please, don't play naive. Why are you always attacking her?"

"I can't stand her," Kwon admitted. "She is so pretentious—the way she dresses, her attitude, her holiness."

"Why don't you just ignore her? Walk away?"

"Because she has that 'made in Japan' tattoo on her forehead. And when you approach her, it flashes 'I'm Japanese and Japanese is better than you.' It pisses me off."

"So you don't like her because she's Japanese? Really?"

"No, it's not a racial thing. It's a matter of the truth. She won't admit the truth about Japan."

"And what is that?"

Kwon paused, letting a silence build. When he finally answered his voice was pensive. "The truth is what I want her to discover."

"And...?"

"It's hard to put into words."

"Well, it looks to me like you're harassing her." Keahi was disappointed in his friend and the disappointment projected in his voice. "And that's the way others see it, too."

"I just want Masako to open her eyes and see the world as it really is." Kwon sighed. "That's all."

"You're full of shit," Keahi said. "You know that, don't you? And *that's* the truth. You keep this up and she will file a complaint. Is that what you want? To have people think you're a racist?"

Kwon stared out the window, thinking hard as they drove past a tired field with grazing horses.

"She's going through life like a horse with blinders on."

Keahi glanced at Kwon. *What in the world is he talking about?* "So what? What does that have to do with you?"

They passed a dilapidated house that needed a coat of paint. A junk car was parked in the front yard and another car, at the side of the house, was half-hidden in tall weeds. Dried shrubs looked like kindling. Fences were unkempt and falling down.

Keahi waited for Kwon to explain further, but he just stared out the window.

Driving through this rural beach community always depressed Keahi. Some of the tour books described the area as picturesque, with a Southeast Asian-like quality. Keahi saw it for what it was: a community that had never recovered when the sugar plantations closed. It was an old, tired, anemic community. People who lived here had a long commute to work—if they worked.

And he was growing impatient with the traffic.

"I think you're harassing her."

Just then the driver in the pickup in front of them threw a paper cup out his window. It blew into the bed of his truck, spun around in a vortex of wind, and then shot out onto the beach side of the road, landing in the weeds.

"What an asshole," Kwon said. "No respect for the *aina*."

Don't change the subject, Keahi thought.

They followed the road another four miles and then made a left turn onto the Pali Hwy and climbed up the mountains into a dense rainforest. Neither of them said a word. Descending, they passed red ginger, which grew wild on both sides of the road.

A few minutes later they turned off the Pali, and in another fifteen minutes they were at the child care center. Keahi tried to turn down a side street next to the center but a policeman stopped him.

"Can I help you?"

Keahi rolled down his dirty window. "We're with the Department of Water, Wind and Sun. I got a call about the explosion?"

"Down the street at the pet store, behind the fire engine," the policeman said. Keahi looked beyond the policeman and down the side street. He saw a lime fire truck parked in the middle of the street. There was barely enough room for the fire truck, certainly not enough room for Keahi's Dodge, too.

"You can park at the child care center," the policeman suggested.

"Thanks."

The officer stepped aside and Keahi drove a short distance down the side street and then turned into the child care center parking lot.

"Oh God, it's the media," Keahi said.

"Where?"

"Over there. See the news van?" Keahi pulled into a slot as far away from the van as possible.

"Crabs with cameras," Kwon said.

"And we look terrible," Keahi said, glancing in the rearview mirror. "A couple of beach bums." He was still wearing his

T-shirt and board shorts and flip-flops; Kwon had on a tank top and Chaps shorts and a pair of tennis shoes.

"We're not dressed for this," Keahi reiterated. "And we don't have any protective equipment."

"We don't have to go in," Kwon said. "Let's just find out what happened. We can come back tomorrow, during work hours."

Keahi thought about that. It seemed reasonable. They'd just take a quick look, in and out. Maybe ask a few questions.

He took a brush out of the storage compartment between the seats and pulled it through his hair; then he looked into the mirror again. He frowned. His hair looked like he had been swimming and his eyes were bloodshot from ocean water and barbecue smoke.

Kwon got out of the car and scrutinized his reflection in the door window. He ran his fingers through his hair. "Maybe no one will recognize us when they see us on the news?"

Keahi frowned at the thought of being on the news. He took a deep breath and exhaled loudly. "Don't bet on it."

He got out of the car and they walked side-by-side apprehensively down the middle of the street towards the lime fire truck and the pet store. He glanced sideways at Kwon. His fused elbow was extended outwards to his side, his arthritic hands were cupped together in front of him, and his shoulders were hunched forward. He had no hips to speak of and his legs sported varicose veins. He was short and thin and his hair was messed up. Keahi suddenly felt an overwhelming empathy for him, a sudden need to protect him. He wanted to put his arm gently around him, pull him close, shield him.

"Oh no!" Keahi groaned. "It's the preschool administrator."

"Where?"

"By the shower tree, talking to the reporters. And I see two shoulder cameras, and that means two camera crews, two television stations." Keahi's stomach turned inside out.

Just then, a tall, wiry man stepped out of the pet store. He walked down the sidewalk, ducked under the yellow tape, and joined the reporters and administrator under the shower tree, between the pet store and the child care center.

"I wonder who the haole is," Keahi said.

"Pet store owner?"

Keahi, with Kwon in tow, walked up to the group cautiously. The shade of the shower tree was cooler, yet Keahi was sweating.

The administrator immediately recognized him. "What the hell happened?" she vented. "Why was there another explosion?"

"I don't know." Keahi shrugged his shoulders.

"You don't know? A mother called me. She asked me if it was safe for her daughter. What am I supposed to tell her? The child care center is safe, but the neighborhood is blowing up?"

The reporters picked up on the anxiety in her voice, which Keahi found very unnerving; they had microphones in their hands.

"Bad luck, just a never-ending stream of bad luck," she said.

"Did something else happen?" Kwon asked.

"Some kids broke in."

"Into the child care center? Was anything stolen?"

"No, nothing. But everything was ransacked. Files were dumped on the floor. It took us hours to reorganize. And now another explosion?"

Keahi watched helplessly as the reporters focused their cameras on him and strategically placed their microphones to catch any sound he might utter.

"I'm sorry to hear that."

He felt overwhelmed, then angry. He glanced at Kwon, who looked as tense as a mongoose facing several snakes.

"In light of a second explosion in the neighborhood, is it safe for the children of Kehena Kare to return to school?" a television reporter asked, sticking a microphone in Keahi's face.

"The fire department and police are here," Keahi answered, as he judged the distance between himself and the front door of the pet store. He decided that it was less than 10 yards away. "They will not allow anyone back into the area until it is safe."

"What is your role in the investigation?" the reporter asked.

"Can we expect more explosions?" the second reporter butted in.

"At this time, I don't know," Keahi said.

"You don't know?" the haole interjected, disbelief in his voice.

"We need to finish our investigation," Keahi said. Then, motioning Kwon to follow him, he pushed past the two reporters and the cameramen and ducked under the yellow tape.

"Could there be another explosion?" the second reporter asked.

"At this time, I don't know," Keahi repeated as he began walking towards the pet store.

The administrator yelled after him. "What am I going to tell the parents? Is it safe for the children? Is there going to be another explosion?"

Keahi didn't stop and he didn't answer. His goal was to get away from the administrator, the reporters and the cameras. Kwon trailed a few steps behind as they scampered down the sidewalk to the front entrance of the pet store, where a policeman stopped them.

The policeman looked Keahi over, his eyes disapproving of the board shorts and slippers.

Keahi adjusted his shorts and smiled. He fished his state ID and driver's license out of a Velcro-sealed back pocket. He wasn't carrying a wallet or money. "We came straight from the beach," he explained. "We had no time to change."

The policeman studied the ID. In small print at the bottom it read "Notice to Civil Authorities: Please permit the EMERGENCY WORKER identified by this card to report to his/her duty station." He compared the photo to Keahi. "All right," the policeman said. "But be careful, there is a lot of broken glass."

Keahi watched as Kwon took out his wallet and fumbled around until he found his state identification card. The picture on the card was off-color and Kwon's face was yellow-green. The hologram on the identification card glinted in the sunlight.

The police stepped aside and Keahi and then Kwon entered the shattered store, stepping onto a bare concrete floor.

"Has the cause been identified?" Keahi asked.

"It wasn't a bomb, if that's what you're wondering," the policeman answered standing at his post by the door.

A voice from the back of the store added, "An electrical vault in the yard exploded. It blew out a breaker box in the storeroom, too." A fireman stepped forward from the back of the large room where aquariums lay on the floor, shattered. He clipped a combustible gas indicator to his belt and extended his hand in greeting to Kwon. After quick introductions, the fireman continued, "It was a flammable substance in a confined space—some kind of explosive gas mixed with oxygen in the underground vault, the power line conduit, and the breaker box. I imagine that the power line sparked. That ignited the explosive mixture, the oxygen and vapors."

"No fire?" Kwon asked. The room lacked the after-smell of a fire. Instead, it smelled like a dirty fish bowl.

"Fire was confined to the breaker box and underground vault. But as you can see, the force of the explosion shattered the aquariums." He glanced at Keahi's slippers and Kwon's sneakers. "Watch your feet."

Sunlight entered the room through the store windows that faced the street and the open front door, illuminating the wet shards of glass glistening on the floor. Aquariums at the back of the store had shattered, too.

Keahi felt something soft under his slipper. He lifted up his foot and saw the crushed body of a small fish.

"I'm glad Toi isn't here. This would break her heart."

He looked closer at the shattered glass and saw dead fish everywhere, their soft, colorful bodies next to sharp glass on gray-painted concrete.

Kwon stepped cautiously to the back of the store and stood in front of a large saltwater aquarium. "Well, at least the fish in this tank survived."

Keahi decided to join him. He walked across the floor, carefully pushing glass and dead fish out of his way with the toe of his slipper. He heard glass snap under heavy black boots as the fireman nonchalantly stepped to the large aquarium, too.

As Keahi got closer to the back of the store, the smell of fish grew stronger. He smelled ammonia from the aquarium water puddled on the floor. It stank.

"That's a damn big tank," Kwon said. "Must be 300 gallons."

The fireman, Kwon and Keahi now stood side-by-side, watching a school of cichlids swim back and forth and round and round.

"It looks homemade," the fireman said.

"Do you think the explosions are related?" Keahi asked Kwon.

"Well . . . I would guess that there is an explosive substance moving underground," Kwon suggested. "Perhaps being carried by a plume of groundwater. If so, then the plume is quite large, or perhaps the plume has divided, or perhaps the plume itself is moving."

"Or we are dealing with two unrelated explosions," Keahi proposed.

"Not likely," Kwon replied. "Both explosions occurred where three properties meet—Club Kesago, the child care center, and this pet store. The property lines converge in the back yards."

"Yes, they do," Keahi agreed. He tapped the shimmering glass to get the attention of the fish. They darted around in the tank, vertical black stripes on gray bodies, with orange markings on their sides and orange-ringed spots near their caudal fins. They were about eight inches long.

He looked carefully at a crack in the top left corner of the tank. It was near the top of the tank and didn't appear to pass all the way through the heavy glass pane.

"Is there an underground utility?" the fireman asked. He had been listening quietly to their conversation. "An underground line that connects all the properties?"

"We already checked the as-builts and saw nothing like that," Keahi said, addressing the fireman. "The utilities are in the front. The building sewers and the water lines run to the middle of the street."

"Perhaps an old, private utility line running across the back of the properties?" the fireman suggested. "Something installed long, long ago?"

"We scanned with a metal detector and found nothing," Keahi said.

"Maybe it's an old clay pipe," the fireman speculated.

"A clay pipe *would* be hard to detect," Kwon acknowledged, raising an eyebrow. "Even with ground-penetrating radar."

Keahi turned his attention again to the fish and tapped the glass harder. The startled fish darted sideways.

"We could rip the property line with a trench cutter," Kwon suggested. "If there's an old line we'd hit it."

"It could be a sand- or gravel-filled trench," the fireman added.

"This smell is overpowering," Keahi said.

"Ammonia from the fish wastes," Kwon said.

"I'll let some fresh air in." The fireman quickly crossed the floor, glass crunching under his heavy black boots, and soon had the back door propped open with a chair.

Keahi tapped the tank again.

"Don't you think those tigers have had enough trauma for one day?" Kwon asked.

"What? Oh, sorry," Keahi replied. He stepped back from the tank.

He now noticed a second crack near the bottom right corner of the tank, not at the top. "I was just thinking . . ."

He felt a breeze pass through the store—in the front door and out the back door. He watched Kwon's bangs blow off his forehead.

"That breeze feels wonder—"

The front door slammed and all three of them jumped straight up. The concrete floor vibrated.

The aquarium exploded.

Kwon never finished his sentence.

While waiting for the ambulance, Keahi wrapped his T-shirt tightly around Kwon's lacerated legs to try and stop the profuse bleeding.

After returning home from the hospital, Keahi took a long hot shower and washed the saltwater and blood off his arms and legs. He was tired, too tired to sleep.

He grabbed a large Foster's Lager, wrapped the can in a brown paper sack, and walked down to the statute of Gandhi in front of the zoo. The statue stood in an open area next to a huge banyan tree. There was space to think and several benches to sit on.

Keahi sat at the foot of the statue and gazed up at the kind face.

"I'm tired, Babu."

He watched a man with a sun-damaged, dark brown face shuffle by, wearing layers of filthy winter clothes, disheveled hair, a stubbled beard, and dirty feet. The man smelled like urine, which reminded Keahi of the aquarium water and fish wastes.

Images of Kwon's lacerated legs raced through his mind.

"Kwon is in the hospital," Keahi said to Gandhi, "Dead fish everywhere."

The man stopped, turned, stared at Keahi.

"What's you got there?" the man mumbled. "You got a bottle?"

"Get," Keahi snapped.

"Where's your aloha?"

"I'll call the police."

"Fuck you, asshole!"

Rebuffed, the man stumbled over to the banyan tree and lay down in the detritus.

Keahi asked Gandhi, "Why am I still working at this job? Little Bill's dead, Pete quit, and now Kwon's in the hospital. I hate my job."

He took another swig of cold beer.

"And why did Little Bill take the picture of the old, rusty, stupid swing set?" Keahi yawned and looked at Gandhi, as if waiting for a reply. He sipped the beer.

"Why such a morbid souvenir? And where is it?"

Keahi finished the beer and walked back to his studio, his mind exploding with questions.

Once back in the kitchen, he threw the empty can into the trashcan. He folded the paper sack and returned it to the cabinet. Then he took another Foster's from the refrigerator, cracked it open and took a long swig.

After that, he called the child care center, hoping the

administrator would still be there. Maybe she was working late, working on damage control.

No answer.

He looked at his alarm clock. It was after midnight! He'd have to wait.

Drinking cold Foster's in a chair on the lanai, he fell asleep.

He awoke at fifteen minutes after five. It was still dark outside and quiet.

He turned on his studio light, found the administrator's cell number in his field notes, waited an hour, and then called her.

Her husband answered and Keahi introduced himself.

"Do you know what time it is?" Pablo's voice was angry.

"Yes, but there is something important I need to ask your wife. May I talk to her?"

Pause.

"Hello," she said.

Keahi heard Pablo curse in the background.

"This is Keahi. Yes, with the Department of Water, Wind and Sun. I'm sorry to bother you so early."

"How is your co-worker?"

"Kwon? He'll be okay."

"I hope so."

"Your husband said he loaned a photograph to Little Bill?"

"Yes, it was a picture of the swing set when it was new."

"My co-worker never gave it back?"

"No, but that's okay."

"Can you send me a copy?"

"No. I don't have a copy."

Keahi thought for a moment. "Was it digital or is there a negative?"

There was a pause. "I don't know. Maybe there is a negative."

"Can I borrow it?"

There was a longer pause. "If I come across it, I'll call you."

"Thanks," Keahi said. "You're going to open today?"

"Any problems with that?"

"No," Keahi said. "But I need to bring a trencher into the playground, so I need access to the area at the back of the playground, at the property line, next to the pet store property."

"Why?"

"To see if there is an old, private utility line or drainage trench between the properties—a conduit for gasoline to travel."

"Good God! Gasoline! Pablo said you'd mentioned gasoline."

"Maybe."

She hung up, abruptly.

Surprised, he set the phone back in its cradle.

He massaged the back of his neck with his fingers and slowly rolled his head side-to-side, yet it gave him no relief from the tension.

"What a mess," he said aloud.

Fatigued from a restless night, he decided to stay at home on sick leave. And then he drank heavily the next two days, missing work.

At 8:35 on the morning of the third day, Keahi entered Jack's office, five minutes late. Jack was seated behind his desk under the painting of the Boston Tea Party.

A television set and VCR player on a cart had been rolled in and pushed up against a wall. A local news report was playing. Keahi was surprised at how old the equipment was.

After Keahi sat down, Jack picked up the remote control off his desk, set the volume to mute, stopped the tape and then set it to rewind. Then he set the remote down and turned his attention to Keahi.

"How is Kwon?" Keahi asked. The day after the explosion, he had been able to reach Kwon in the hospital on his cell phone, but Kwon had been heavily medicated and seemed confused about his condition.

"Bad shape. His legs are messed up. Deep lacerations. He lost a lot of blood." Jack paused. "And you? Are you feeling better?"

"Not a scratch." Keahi was aware that Jack was looking at him long and hard.

"I have reassigned the case to Santos," Jack said, "effective immediately."

"What?" Keahi was stunned.

"Have you seen the news reports?"

"No."

"Well, a lot has happened during the last few days," Jack said.

Neither said a word as they waited for the tape to rewind. During the silence Keahi focused his attention on the paining of the Boston Tea Party, trying to avoid eye contact with Jack.

Three ships were in the dark painting. Aboard one, beneath a confusing array of ropes and rigging and three masts, in the glow of yellow light from black lanterns, a group of angry haoles were masquerading as Indians: white faces painted black with coal dust, goose feathers atop their heads, holding hatchets instead of tomahawks. One haole was chopping at a square wooden box with a long-handled axe. Others were heaving split and open boxes overboard into the sea. Alongside the ship were a rowboat and two men, one seated in the bow holding a black lantern aglow with yellow light, the other standing astride the boat holding an oar overhead. Both were dressed up as Indians. Boxes of tea floated around the rowboat, destroyed.

Keahi felt drained of energy. He was dehydrated, having forgotten to take his aspirin, water, and apple-banana remedy before falling asleep on the lanai last night. Now he felt miserable. Three days and four nights had passed in a blur of inactivity.

When the tape reached the end, Jack fast-forwarded it to a preset numerical starting point. Then he walked around his desk and sat in a chair next to Keahi. Keahi moved his gaze from the picture to the television set, still avoiding eye contact. They both readjusted their seats to get a comfortable view of the television screen, and then Jack pushed play and the VCR hummed.

Keahi appeared on the screen and Jack punched up the volume.

"In light of a second explosion in the neighborhood, is it safe for the children of Kehena Kare to return to class?" a television reporter asked.

"At this time, I don't know," Keahi replied.

"You don't know?" The child care administrator appeared on the screen, upset. "A mother called me at home. She asked me if it was safe for her daughter. What am I supposed to tell her?"

"At this time, I don't know," Keahi repeated. They showed a close-up of his face and his eyes looked tired and bloodshot.

"Could there be another explosion?" a reporter asked.

They showed another close-up of Keahi's face. He looked overwhelmed and angry. Then they showed Kwon and Keahi turning their backs on the owner of the child care center, ducking under the yellow tape, and walking away.

As they walked quickly and deliberately away, the child care administrator yelled after them "What am I going to tell the parents? Is it safe for the children? Is there going to be another explosion?"

The tape showed Kwon following a few steps behind Keahi. He glanced nervously back at the cameras.

Then there was a clear shot of Keahi from the back as he was greeted and stopped by the policeman at the front door of the pet store. Keahi was wearing his board shorts and slippers. His beachwear contrasted sharply with the policeman's pressed uniform and professional demeanor. Keahi adjusted his board shorts as Kwon produced an identification card. He then entered the pet store followed by Keahi.

The next shot was a picture of Kwon on a gurney, being rolled out of the pet store; the sheets covering the lower half of his body were red, soaked in blood. He was grimacing in pain. Keahi was walking beside the gurney, without a shirt, wearing only board shorts and flip-flops. He looked a mess, a disgrace.

Keahi, now watching the tape, was keenly aware that neither Kwon nor he had been wearing the minimum required personal protective equipment—hard hat, long pants, long-sleeved shirt, and steel toe non-slip boots—for entering the site.

Then the tape showed the paramedics hoisting Kwon and the gurney into the ambulance.

The tape cut to the expression on the face of the preschool administrator; disbelief and fear were in her eyes.

Then the tape cut back to Keahi. He hopped into the back of the ambulance, losing one of his slippers, which fell to the black asphalt. One of the paramedics picked up the slipper and handed it to him, then closed the back door of the ambulance.

The last shot showed the ambulance pulling away with the child care center in the background.

Jack stopped the tape.

Keahi slumped back into the guest chair. He wished it would swallow him up.

"Santos is telling everyone that you botched the investigation."

"That's ridiculous!" Keahi protested, his voice quivering with emotion; he had to consciously control his hands to stop their shaking. Carefully and slowly he said, "Is this the same guy who refused to let me delineate the extent of the plume?"

"Well," Jack replied, "if it makes you feel any better Santos is also telling everyone that I'm at fault, too. And he's put a unique slant on the meeting we had in the courtyard. Remember the meeting? Well, yesterday the union filed a grievance on his behalf. They're saying that I failed to negotiate before changing work conditions. So you see, he's trying to make us both look incompetent."

"Also," Jack continued, "at the end of the day yesterday, I received a call from a lawyer representing the owner of the pet store. She requested copies of everything we have on this case. In particular, she requested copies of your files, Keahi." Jack handed Keahi a phone message with the lawyer's name and phone number.

"I'll call her back," Keahi said. "I'll prepare the file and set up a time for her to come down to review it."

"No," Jack said. "Prepare the file and then turn it over to our Deputy Attorney. Let him call and set up the appointment. You are not to talk with their attorney. You understand?"

"Yes, I understand." Keahi's voice was heavy and filled with resignation.

"Also . . ."

"What?" Keahi asked.

"We are getting calls from angry parents."

"Why?"

"The center shut down."

"Really? When I last talked to the administrator, she said the center would be open."

"Well, I heard from her husband, I believe his name is Pablo? They went in the morning after the explosion, but they didn't open up. Seems the press was waiting for them, to get reaction from the parents as they dropped off their kids."

"Good grief," Keahi mumbled. In his mind he pictured a tangle of crabs crawling over each other, trying to get to a raw chicken neck tied to the wire frame of a crab trap.

"Did you call them at six o'clock in the morning?"

"I did, yes."

"Well, they complained about that, too."

"I see."

Keahi could read the expression on Jack's face. It said, "What's the matter with you?" Keahi didn't respond.

Then Jack added, shaking his head, "And you asked permission to trench along their back property line?"

"Yes."

"Well, that also upset Pablo. Now he's worrying about his personal liability."

"Lawyers will only make the investigation more difficult."

"Well, that won't be your problem now, well it? Like I said, as of this morning, you are officially off the case." Jack paused, took a deep breath and exhaled as if tired. "It's Santos's case now."

Damn! Keahi thought. "It can't get any worse than that," he said, mostly to himself.

"That reminds me," Jack said, "the Hawaii Office of Safety and Health called this morning. They are investigating Kwon's accident. They want to know our standard operating procedures for responding to an emergency. They asked me if I thought a swim suit and slippers were standard protective equipment."

Keahi slumped further into the chair. He guessed that HIOSH inspectors had seen the news report and would request a video copy from the news station. Perhaps they already had.

Normally he kept his hard hat, boots, long pants and a long-sleeve shirt in his car, but this time he had forgotten them. He had not expected to be called on a weekend, especially on a Sunday afternoon.

"I need our standard operating procedures on my desk before noon." The tone of Jack's voice was not happy. "And I also need a full written report documenting everything that happened out there. I need that by noon, too. After lunch we will sit down with our Deputy Attorney. Any questions?"

Keahi shook his head wearily.

When Keahi returned to his cubicle, he found someone had placed a copy of the morning *Honolulu Advertiser* on his chair. The cover story was from three days ago and it was the explosion at the pet store. In the cover photo Keahi sat in the ambulance holding his slipper in his right hand, looking startled and frantic, his hands wet with Kwon's blood. The photo was Pulitzer quality.

CHAPTER FOUR

Lim was ferrying the last of his co-workers from the boat harbor to Jack's beach picnic on Kipapa Sandbar. His new catamaran held Toi, Masako and Keahi comfortably.

Keahi was seated aft, watching Lim, trying to decide whether or not he liked him. He knew Lim was born and raised on Mainland China. He also knew Lim had earned a degree in the United States, but in what he wasn't sure; nevertheless, Lim's training had been good enough to land him a position as hydrologist in the Water Well Unit. And now he knew that Lim had a fast, new catamaran. Other than that, Keahi knew nothing personal about him.

"Nice boat," Keahi ventured.

"It's small but fun." Lim smiled. "My dream is to own a thirty-three footer."

"You've got an expensive hobby."

"Sailing is in my blood," Lim said proudly. "My ancestors were Taiwanese pirates who fought the invading Manchus." He laughed loudly. "That's what my wife says, anyway."

"Pirates?" Toi's voice was high-pitched. "Pirates aren't funny."

"Captain Sparrow was funny," Lim said, chuckling. "Especially in *Pirates of the Caribbean*."

"But I was *attacked* by pirates."

"No way!" Lim exclaimed as the pontoon slapped a wave. "Pirates? Attacked *you*?"

"In the Gulf of Thailand."

"No way!"

The boat became quiet as everyone waited for Toi to explain, but instead she just stared off into the bay. For some moments it was quiet, except for the pontoons rhythmically slapping the waves.

Her memories must still be painful, Keahi thought, so he changed the subject: "Kwon got his stitches out."

"How many?"

"Three hundred and something."

"My God! Can he walk?"

"Yes, but it's painful."

"How awful!" Toi exclaimed, casting off her memories of the pirates and returning to the present.

"Sounds like a shark mauled him," Lim said.

Keahi saw the color drain from Toi's face and he instantly regretted bringing up Kwon's physical condition.

"It's too bright on your boat," Keahi said.

"What?" Lim asked. "Too bright?"

"The sun," Keahi explained. "The surgeon ordered Kwon to stay out of the sunlight or risk scarring. He was already sensitive to the sun, you know."

Lim looked at Keahi with a curious expression, so Keahi explained. "He takes an anti-malarial drug that makes him sensitive to the sun. I forget the name of the drug, but he takes it to keep his arthritis in remission."

"So *that's* his beef with the Freon smugglers," Masako suggested, a touch of condescension in her voice.

Keahi frowned. "Yes, Freon damages the ozone layer and that allows in harmful rays." Keahi looked at the sunlight sparkling on the water and squinted his eyes. "And yes, his medication makes him especially sensitive to ultraviolet rays."

"And I thought his motives were altruistic," Masako said sarcastically.

"Nothing wrong with self-preservation," Keahi countered. "He gets a gold shot once a month and a shot of some other drug every two weeks. It's called metho-something-or-another."

"His arthritis is that bad?" Toi asked.

"Haven't you noticed his hands?" Keahi asked.

"Yes."

"And his elbow?"

"It's cocked outward."

"Like a chicken wing," Masako interjected.

"It's almost fused at the joint," Keahi said, the tone of his voice admonishing. "He can barely bend it."

"And now his legs . . ." Toi added.

Keahi winced. The memory of the aquarium breaking and the glass slashing muscle to the bone was still vivid. "Touché."

And now Hawaii's Occupational Safety and Health Department was investigating. Keahi sighed heavily. Safety inspectors from HIOSH had questioned him and everyone else involved in the response. In fact, Keahi expected them to release their report soon and he had no doubts that it would reflect poorly on him. The Department would be fined and he would be reprimanded. But that bothered him less than the fact that he had failed to prevent the accident, had stayed drunk for several days, and consequently had even failed to visit Kwon in the hospital.

As they approached the sandbar, Lim put the catamaran to wind, lowered the mainsail, and steered towards a submerged bar under the power of the jib. A few moments later he ran aground where Jack was standing in ankle-deep water. Everyone jumped off and pulled the catamaran higher onto the sand, making sure that it was well-beached.

Jack helped them unload: first, two heavy plastic chests filled with picnic food, then two dark blue folding chairs, one Toi's and the other Masako's, and last, a large umbrella—bright yellow, blue and crimson red. Keahi stuck the umbrella in the sand and opened it and set the chairs in its shade.

Masako and Toi plopped into the seats and the back legs of the chairs disappeared into the soft, wet sand. Their knees shot up into the air and they screamed.

Everyone roared with laughter.

Masako tried to push herself out of the chair but only sank deeper. Toi grabbed the umbrella and tried to pull herself up, and it crashed down on top of them. They screamed as the seat of their pants got wet.

Keahi pulled them to their feet.

"The tide is rising," Jack said, laughing. "Soon we will all be wet."

"And my catamaran will float free," Lim added.

"So let's eat and enjoy ourselves while we can." Jack leaned over and opened the chests; one contained hot lunches, the other, cold sodas. He started passing out plate lunches—huli huli chicken and two scoops of rice and macaroni salad, purchased earlier in the day from a local fundraiser. Masako, Keahi, Lim, Toi and about a dozen of their colleagues gathered around, took a plate lunch, grabbed sodas.

When Jack handed Keahi a warm paper plate filled with food and covered with shiny foil, Keahi blurted, "You know, the department is really messed up!"

"Messed up?" Jack was taken aback. "What do you mean?"

"Broken. Messed up."

Jack raised an eyebrow.

Keahi wanted to say, *I know what's going on.* But instead he said, "I'm just frustrated. Like everyone else."

He knew, as everyone knew, that Santos and the union were making frivolous complaints against Jack. He also heard the rumors that upper management had chosen not to give Jack their support. In fact, upper management was deliberately withholding their support. And that, in particular, was becoming a problem—not only for Jack but also for Keahi, because it was empowering Santos. And that was making Keahi's life miserable.

Santos had always been a lazy and slow supervisor. He was a paper pusher who got very little real work done. But now everyone was seeing another side of his personality. Since his meeting with Jack in the courtyard, he had become increasingly paranoid, defensive, and argumentative. And his pages of complaints against Jack were increasingly filled with half-truths and misrepresentations.

Keahi imagined how difficult it would be to defend against such ranting, especially if upper management wouldn't acknowledge that the complaints against Jack were from a disgruntled employee with a personal vendetta, and perhaps even a mental problem. Yeah, Santos was like a whiny kid throwing a temper tantrum, demanding attention, taking up Jack's time and energy. Jack was trapped in a no-win situation. Everyone seemed to know that, and it was putting a damper on their work and even on today's picnic. One disgruntled employee...

Keahi walked away and sat on the edge of Lim's catamaran, next to Lim and close to where Masako and Toi had moved their chairs. He sensed that Jack was watching him. He positioned the cotton material of his Bermudas between the hot paper plate and his bare skin. Glancing in Jack's direction, he saw that Jack was handing out plate lunches to their colleagues.

Boy, that was stupid of me, Keahi thought.

Resting on the edge of the catamaran, he reviewed what he knew about Jack. The bottom line: Jack was his own person. He was friendly with the people who reported to him, went on picnics with them, fed them. And amazingly, he embraced change, such as converting the courtyard at work into a meeting area.

Keahi shook his head. It was only a matter of time, he suspected, before other disgruntled staff joined Santos in his personal attack. Keahi sighed.

Once Jack passed out the last lunch, he grabbed one for himself and stood an equal distance from Keahi and Lim, who were seated on the catamaran, and Masako and Toi, who were seated in their wet and sandy chairs, forming a triangle.

"So tell me, Keahi," Jack said, pulling the aluminum foil off his plate lunch, "what is broken?"

Keahi wanted to talk about Santos; however, he knew that this wasn't the proper place or time. His outburst was one of the few times that his emotions had gotten the better of him. Instead of talking about Santos's growing paranoia, he said, "It's all messed up." Then he shook his head and gazed out on Kaneohe Bay. He saw nothing but mudflats. The bay was heavily silted from freshwater runoff that had carried topsoil, vegetation, and trash from a dozen tributary streams.

"Well," Jack pursued, "what's messed up?"

"I don't know," Keahi mumbled, thinking, *Santos is not doing his job as a supervisor. He's not investigating the explosion. He's not doing a thing but writing complaints against you!*

Jack turned to Toi, seated next to Masako. "What do you think?"

"Too much red tape?" Toi suggested.

"Red tape?" Jack nodded. "Yes, I suppose there is a labyrinth of unending, unyielding, bureaucratic edict."

"We need more flexibility," Toi added. "Everything is so rigid. We are so rule-bound. There is a policy and procedure for everything. The whole system is unfriendly."

Keahi thought about his great-aunt and what she would say to that. He volunteered, jokingly, "Everything revolves around the governor's belly button."

Jack laughed. "So what can we do about it?" He looked around. No eye contact. No answers.

"Well then, I guess we can't do much," he said with an exaggerated sigh.

He turned to Keahi and qualified his statement: "In fact, I'm not sure that we can do anything about it."

"Then why talk about it?" Keahi snapped back, feeling a mixture of anger and frustration.

"But you are the one who brought it up," Jack said. "You are the unhappy bureaucrat. Not me."

Keahi winced. "What I want," he blurted out, "is to prevent another explosion. How can I do that when my hands and feet are tied?"

"Well, I suppose you could get angry," Jack said.

Keahi was shocked by Jack's suggestion.

"You may be a bureaucrat, Keahi, but at least you're an American bureaucrat."

"What does that mean?"

"Exercise your rights."

Masako snorted, nervously.

"You mean go to the union? File a grievance?"

"No, no," Jack replied. "I'm not talking about the power that you have placed in someone else's hands. I'm talking about the power that you have. I'm talking about—"

"Power?" Keahi interrupted.

"Yes, power," Jack said. "Real power."

"I don't understand," Keahi said.

Jack studied his own hands for a minute. They were the hands of an old man. He then looked into Keahi's eyes and said," Keahi, surely you understand that Santos is responsible for investigating the cause of the explosions, right? He is the supervisor of the unit that is conducting the investigation. So either Santos or his staff—other than you—is expected to perform the investigation. Why? Because it is his job. But regarding the bureaucracy at the department," Jack continued, leaning forward, "Perhaps I can help you with that."

"How?" Keahi asked.

"What did Gandhi do after he was thrown off the train in South Africa for being an Indian and for sitting in the white man's car?"

Keahi was astounded that Jack made reference to Gandhi. Yet on a gut level it seemed to be applicable. Keahi answered: "He sat down on the platform at the train station and he studied the problem."

"Well," Jack said. "Here we are, all of us, on this little sandbar, eating barbecued chicken and macaroni salad, sitting and thinking about how to solve our problems. So let me ask you: do you think one public servant can make a difference?" He smiled and then added, "Even if he is just a bureaucrat?"

Keahi didn't answer glibly. Instead, he reflected seriously on Jack's question. Why had Gandhi reacted the way that he had? Why, of all people, was Gandhi the one who stood up? What was he thinking?

"Isn't a team better than just one person?" Toi asked.

"A team of public servants?" Jack reiterated the question, changing it slightly.

"Yes. Gandhi acted by himself," Toi said. "But wouldn't a team of public servants have a better chance of succeeding than just one person acting alone?"

"What would this team do?"

"Find ways to improve the department," Toi suggested.

"Yes, that would be a worthy goal," Masako said, quickly agreeing with Toi. "Change the bureaucracy."

Jack smiled at Masako and Toi. He rubbed his beardless chin.

"Would you give a team like that the autonomy to make changes?" Lim asked.

Everyone looked at Lim. Until this moment he had been quiet, listening to the conversation. *He's been looking for an angle*, Keahi thought, intuitively.

Jack studied Lim's face and then replied, "Perhaps."

Jack then turned to Masako and asked her, "Would you be willing to be on the team, Masako?"

"I'd need more time to think about it," she said.

Actually, she needs more time to figure out what everyone else wants, Keahi thought. *Then she will know how to answer.*

"Toi," Jack asked. "Would you be willing to be on the team?"

"I think so," Toi replied. She glanced at Keahi, seeking his approval. Their eyes met and Keahi shrugged his shoulders.

"Maybe," Toi said, modifying her response.

"Well, it's about time something happened around here," Lim chimed in again.

Keahi focused on Lim. He still hadn't decided whether or not he liked him.

"How about you, Keahi?" Jack asked, returning the discussion full circle, back to Keahi. "Would you be willing to serve on this team?"

More work! Keahi's brain yelled. But he thought about it, taking his time. It was a big decision. If he said yes, he would be committing himself to working towards changing a bureaucracy, which he considered impossible. He thought,

It would probably be easier to take on the British Empire, like Gandhi did, than to take on a bureaucracy. But something has to change!

"You can count me in," he said to Jack, surprising himself.

"Good! It's time you guys took ownership of your jobs."

Keahi wasn't sure what Jack meant by that, taking ownership of your jobs, but he did like the idea of a team working together to improve things.

"Who else wants to be on the team?" Jack asked.

"I'm in," Toi said.

"Well, count me in, too," Masako said. "Let's do it."

The rest of their colleagues on the sandbar were silent and picked at their macaroni salads.

"Some advice," Jack said to Keahi, Toi and Masako. "Make your team diverse. Select at least one person from each of the divisions, land, air and water. And you have my permission to do whatever is legal and ethical to reach your goal."

"And Keahi," Jack added.

"Yes?"

"Santos and the union will oppose you."

After Keahi and Toi and Masako were seated, Lim pushed the bow of his catamaran off the sandbar, waded out into waist-deep water, and waited for the wind to swing the stern. When the bow was head to wind, he climbed aboard and hoisted the mainsail, then bellowed instructions. The novice crew obeyed.

Carefully avoiding shallow coral heads, they sailed into deeper water. Lim let the sails fill and the catamaran raced faster and faster until she was leaning on one pontoon, the other slapping and skipping on the water.

"What do you guys think about Jack?" Masako asked as the catamaran bobbed up and down.

"He's an original," Keahi said. "One of a kind."

"Can we trust him?"

Keahi thought, *He already knows our strengths and weaknesses because he took the time to get to know each of us. He listened to us, individually. And when we grew tired of talking, he continued to listen. He knows how much I respect Gandhi, obviously. I just hope he understands Santos and upper management, too.* He said, "What do we have to lose?"

"What does *he* have to lose?" Lim interjected. "I mean, he's an old guy. He can afford to take risks. In fact, he's supposed to take risks—he's the Head of Department. We, on the other hand, we have a lot to lose. I mean . . . this team thing . . . if it doesn't work it will hurt our careers. It won't hurt him."

They were quiet for a minute while everyone thought about that. Then Toi asked, "Who should we recruit?"

"How about Kwon?" Keahi suggested.

Masako inhaled through clenched teeth, making a hissing sound and tilting her head. "Kwon? Why in the *world* would you recruit Kwon? You know how I feel about him!"

"Because of his analytical skills," Keahi explained. "He has a special gift, an ability to look at a set of data and detect trends, patterns, problems. He has the ability to ask the right question."

"Special gift?" Masako asked. "Right. He has a gift for offending people. He offends me. I think he's obnoxious. A racist."

"Obnoxious? Yes." Keahi said. "A racist? No." Keahi looked at Masako and saw disbelief in her eyes. "Kwon says what he thinks, but he's not a racist."

"I heard that he's really good with numbers, too," Toi volunteered.

Immediately, a blank expression covered Masako's face.

The catamaran heeled and Toi crossed over and sat next to Keahi to balance the boat.

Masako stared at them in disbelief, her eyes showing surprise and pain. Keahi read it clearly.

"I know that you don't like Kwon," he said to her. "But you need to look beyond that. You need to look at what the team needs. He has a lot to offer."

"Keahi," Masako said, her voice cracking, "I can't work with Kwon."

"What if I talk to him?"

"That won't help."

"Enough," Lim interjected. "Let's put it to a vote. All in favor of including Kwon say aye."

Toi, Lim and Keahi said, "Aye."

"All opposed say nay."

Masako said, "Nay."

"The ayes have it," Lim said. "Three to one. The majority rules."

The catamaran was heeling well over. One hull bounced high out of the water, way up in the air. Lim joined Toi and Keahi, opposite Masako, to balance the boat.

Masako shifted her body and the catamaran bounced higher in the water. She sat alone, her eyes like tide pools. The catamaran was close to flipping.

The nine members of the new team sat around the rectangular table at their first meeting. Keahi and Lim sat at opposite ends. Kwon was on Keahi's right, wearing shorts. His legs were wrapped in bandages and tucked safely under the table. His aloha shirt was characteristically gaudy with red parrots and palm trees. Masako and Toi were seated next to each other near the middle, across from Kwon. Four others were also present, each from a different unit.

Keahi started the meeting with an icebreaker. "Let's do a round robin and introduce ourselves. And share one thing that we'd change if we were the Head of Department for a day."

"I'll start. My name is Keahi. I'm an emergency event coordinator. And if I was the Head of Department for a day, I'd inspect the local labs that we use." Keahi had been upset ever since Santos had given him the business card for Kalele Lab and had insisted he use them. Why couldn't he choose the lab he wanted? Frustrated, he had raised the concern with Kwon, who jumped on the problem and suggested that they check out all the labs, including Kalele Lab.

"Your turn Kwon," Keahi said, starting the round robin counterclockwise.

"My name is Kwon. I'm a permit writer in the Air Unit. And I agree with Keahi. Our decisions can only be as good as the information we receive. So I think we need to inspect the labs, too. We need to make sure they are giving us accurate data."

"Is something wrong with the labs?" Masako spoke up, challenging Kwon.

"I don't know." Her challenge unnerved Kwon and he had to clear his voice. "Most are probably doing a good job. But we don't know, do we?"

"Kwon's right," Keahi said. "What if one is cutting corners?"

"Why do you think that?" Masako asked.

Keahi had no answer, just frustration and pent-up anger against Santos. *I just don't like being told what lab to use.*

"Well, it's obvious, isn't it?" Keahi said, addressing his question to everyone at the table. He was bluffing because he didn't have the science background to defend his suggestion.

A young woman dressed in a white lab coat introduced herself as a supervisor in the department's laboratory and said, "I think the commercial labs are doing a good job, but unless we check them, they are a black box."

"A black box?" Masako asked.

"A sample goes in the front door and a report comes out the back, but you don't know what happened in the lab."

"And no one knows?" Masako asked.

"I recently hired a lab tech who worked in a commercial lab and she told me horror stories. Seventy hour weeks. Old equipment that wouldn't calibrate. New methods modified for ancient machines."

"Where did she work?" Lim asked.

"I shouldn't tell."

All eyes around the table focused on her.

"I mean, I don't have first-hand knowledge."

"Come on," Lim said. "If you can't trust your team, who can you trust?" He smiled.

"Well," the lab supervisor hesitated, "no, I shouldn't say anything. Not without proof. And that's exactly what we need. Good information, solid data."

Keahi noted that Kwon smiled at the lab supervisor, and she returned his smile. *Looks like Kwon has found a kindred spirit*, he thought. He couldn't help but smile, too. *A couple of data junkies?*

"So let me see if I understand your concern," Masako said. "The decisions we make are based on laboratory reports. If the data in the reports are bad, the decisions we make are bad."

"No, our decisions are not bad," Kwon said, correcting Masako in front of everyone. "We make the best decisions we can, but our decisions may be based on data of questionable quality."

Masako glared at Kwon. "Same—"

"Everyone makes the best decisions they can," Keahi interjected, hoping to diffuse the growing tension. "I just think we need a better process for choosing the labs we use."

"Does it really make a difference?" Masako asked, directing her question to the lab supervisor.

"Yes, it does," the middle-aged woman replied. "The labs we use should have a quality assurance and quality control plan. And they should have the proper equipment."

"We should have a certification program," Kwon added.

"I can't believe what I'm hearing," Masako said. "We formed this team to reduce bureaucracy, and now you guys are talking about starting up a certification program? Are you nuts? I thought our goal was to eliminate red tape and improve efficiency, not create more bureaucracy."

Masako, you're right, Keahi thought. *But this is something personal between Santos and me. I want to inspect Kalele Lab.*

He nodded to Toi and said, "Toi, you're next. Let's finish our introductions. Then let's elect a team leader. Okay?"

The icebreaker continued and, after they completed the round robin, they unanimously elected Toi as their first team leader, which she graciously accepted. The team needed a cornerstone, and Toi was the one person everyone trusted to play by the rules, to be conscientious, to be fair.

Keahi turned the meeting over to her. Her first action was to establish a set of ground rules.

After that, Toi lead the team as they discussed which bureaucratic conundrum to tackle. Keahi made a motion that they pursue the lab issue and the lab supervisor seconded his motion. Masako complained that inspecting the labs would only make the department's bureaucracy worse, not better. A heated discussion followed.

Eventually, the team voted the lab certification as the hot issue they would tackle because everyone made decisions based on lab data. Masako voted against the project, casting the only no vote.

Her vote disappointed Keahi.

The team spent the next hour discussing how to inspect the labs. Because of Masako's continued outspoken opposition, the team finally decided against inspections. Instead, they decided to use performance evaluation samples: that is, they would hire a mainland lab to send chemical samples of known quality to all the labs who did work for the department.

"How would that work?" Toi asked the lab supervisor.

"It's a relatively ordinary procedure," the lab supervisor replied. "We send the mainland lab empty sample bottles and our labels and forms. They will add chemicals to water or soil samples, return them to us, and then we will deliver the samples to the local labs. The local labs will think that we collected the samples in the field. They will analyze the samples, business as usual, and then they will send us a lab report. We forward their lab reports to the mainland lab, and they will compare the lab report to the actual concentrations of chemicals they put in our samples. Then the mainland lab will give us a performance evaluation report on each lab."

"So we will know if a lab is cooking their data?" Toi asked.

"Yes," the lab supervisor said. "If a lab is reporting false data, we'll find it."

"Who is going to sell this idea to upper management?" Masako asked, still grumbling.

"I would be willing to spearhead the effort," Keahi volunteered. "Kwon could—"

Lim interrupted. "You will sell upper management on the idea? I thought upper management was investigating *your* performance?"

Masako couldn't help but bark out a laugh.

Keahi started to defend himself, but then stopped. Explaining the HIOSH investigation and what happened at the pet store wouldn't help him gain control of the lab project. Lim had neutralized him, deftly. *Why?* Keahi wondered.

"If you want the project, Lim," Keahi said. "You can have it."

"Is that okay with everyone else?" Lim asked. He looked around the table.

Keahi also glanced at everyone. They all appeared largely indifferent; as long as it was someone else's responsibility, they appeared happy to see the project move forward. No one wanted more work.

This team is going to be a bust, Keahi thought, sadly. He wondered if Jack would be disappointed. If he would even care. Why should he? What's the benefit to him?

The team voted and decided that Lim and the lab supervisor would coordinate the investigation. They would report back to the team when they had results.

Then Lim made a request: "We need to keep this project confidential."

Toi agreed: "On this island, news travels fast."

Lim suggested: "What is said in this room should stay in this room."

The team unanimously agreed, declared the investigation confidential, and agreed that a breach of confidentiality would be a serious offense.

After Toi closed the meeting, Keahi approached Lim. "I'd appreciate it if you would keep me posted. Let me know what you find out."

"You'll know when everyone else does," Lim replied, his voice toneless.

What a passive, materialistic, self-promoter, Keahi concluded. *Yes, nasty.*

CHAPTER FIVE

KEAHI WATCHED HIS 18-YEAR-OLD NEPHEW Liko comb his thick black hair, adjust his U2 Vertigo T-shirt, and hitch up his just-below-the-knee shorts in front of the large koa wood mirror. It was Liko's summer vacation before his senior year. He had just returned to Hawaii and was staying with Keahi in his studio again, as he had done the previous summer.

Liko appeared stronger, not as soft as last summer; his biceps and triceps were less fatty, no more wave. "Have you been lifting weights?"

"Four times a week." Liko admired himself framed in the mirror. "I'm looking good, huh?"

"You lost some baby fat."

"Baby fat?"

"Your girlfriend should like that."

Liko smiled, suddenly aware of his narcissism and that Keahi was teasing him. "No, no, no—I'm meeting a friend."

Keahi returned the smile.

"Just someone I met last summer."

Keahi's smile broadened.

"Just someone I've been writing to."

"Auwe! She must be special!"

Keahi waited for a reply, but Liko volunteered nothing more beyond his blushing ears.

"Listen," Liko said, "I need a summer job. Do you have any ideas?"

Keahi looked at him—really looked at him. He had changed. When he returned to his mom's trailer park just outside Las Vegas last summer, he was a six foot three, 300-pound hurt puppy carrying his tail between his legs. But now he was lifting weights and had lost weight. And now he cared about his appearance. No more baggy T-shirts. No more baseball hat worn backwards. And no more white socks with leather slippers. Now he had a girlfriend. And he wanted a job! What next?

Keahi grinned from ear to ear. "I'll check around and see what I can find. I guess a man with a girlfriend needs spending money?"

They both chuckled their distinctive family chuckle. Liko looked at himself in the mirror, messed up his short black hair, and then neatly combed it again. He seldom cursed his family genes anymore.

Keahi thought that he seemed a bit nervous, though. Maybe a bit anxious. "Is this the girl you met last year at Queen's Beach—I mean San Souci?"

"Maybe is. Maybe ain't."

Liko met Toi in front of the chambered nautilus exhibit inside the Waikiki Aquarium at 3:30pm, as they had arranged; Toi volunteered at the Waikiki Aquarium on weekends and after her regular job at the Department of Water, Wind and Sun.

"You look great," Toi said. "You've lost weight!"

"Yeah," Liko said, pleased that she had noticed. He had written to her about his weight training at school, but he could tell by her reaction that she was surprised. Even though he was still over 250 pounds, his stomach was leaner, his waist, narrower.

They hugged. He kissed her shyly on her right cheek. Then he took her small hand.

She squeezed his hand, affectionately, but immediately released it. She then escorted him into the lobby, stopping in front of the gift shop.

He felt lighter than air.

"How old are you?' Toi asked.

"Eighteen. Why?"

"I'm over thirty."

"So?"

"I just wanted you to know."

They exchanged smiles.

"Liko, there is something you have to see."

He followed closely as she led him out the back door of the aquarium and into the bright sunlight, temporarily blinding him. He squinted, shielding his eyes with his hand. They turned right and walked a few yards, and then stopped in front of an outdoor exhibit.

"What in the world are they?" Liko asked, his face shining with amazement.

"Monk seals!" A low-tempered excitement was present in her voice.

"Incredible! I've never seen anything like them."

The three monk seals were huge, friendly looking creatures with brown fur and sleek, blubbery bodies. The closest seal gargled. It had a sad, puppy face, a smooth head with no ears—only holes in the sides of its head—long whiskers and big brown almond-shaped eyes, which appeared full of wonder and curiosity. Liko pointed out the five digits on each front flipper. He sensed hidden strength—powerful muscles beneath a thick layer of blubber.

"They are clumsy on land, but graceful in the water. They can dive 1,500 feet!"

"Wow! That's deeper than the Bowfin." Liko shivered remembering how claustrophobic he had felt last summer when he and Keahi toured the vintage WWII submarine at Pearl Harbor.

As they watched, a monk seal slid into the water and swam gracefully around the concrete swimming hole while the other two lay lazily on the concrete deck. Their enclosure was small and concrete and not very interesting. Liko thought they appeared bored.

Together Toi and he watched the monk seal swim in circles, using its hind flipper like a fish's tail and its small front flippers to maneuver. After a few minutes, the seal stopped swimming and lay on the bottom of the tank.

"You learned to swim?"

"Yes, I did." Liko guessed that watching the monk seal swim and then sink to the bottom of the tank had jogged her memory about his near-disastrous dive last year. *I'm no longer a dog-paddler.* He smiled at her.

"You took lessons?"

"At school. A swim class. And I joined the swim team."

Toi's expression was unmasked happiness.

In fact, Liko had become a fanatical swimmer. Almost every day, after school, he had practiced with the junior swim team, swimming laps, resting, then swimming more laps. The pool was closed on holidays; hence, holidays were the only days he didn't practice.

"Do they bite?"

"Yes. They'll bite you. They'll defend their pups, but they're not as aggressive as sea lions, like the sea lions in San Francisco. Sea lions are related to bears; monk seals are related to otters. They're more passive."

"I bet they could throw their weight around if they wanted to," Liko said, grinning. "Their size alone could be dangerous."

"Their cousins, the Caribbean seals, were passive, too; they were clubbed to death and are now extinct. They have relatives in the Mediterranean but that's about it. They're the last of their kind."

"They must eat a lot of fish?"

"And squid and eels and octopus and spiny lobster tails."

"The local fishermen must hate them!"

The monk seal was still lying on the bottom of the concrete tank. It hadn't moved.

"Doesn't he have to breathe?" Liko asked.

They waited, curious, and after another three minutes the seal finally surfaced, hoisted itself onto the concrete skirting, and lay in the bright sun. Then it belched.

They both laughed, Liko chuckling.

The afternoon sun was intense, so they soon returned to the inside exhibits. While Liko's eyes adjusted, Toi escorted him to bleacher-style seats, where they sat in front of a large indoor aquarium. Black-tipped sharks glided in front of them, back and forth.

"Sharks once surrounded me." She enunciated each word clearly and rhythmically. "I was on a refugee boat. Pirates seized our boat and I had to jump into the ocean. I saw the sharks. I saw them before I jumped. But I had to jump. A pirate was chasing me. I was so scared!"

She stared at the sharks gliding in the aquarium.

"The sharks didn't attack. I don't know why. Maybe it was because the pirates had thrown junk into the water—baskets and pillaged suitcases." She looked intently into his eyes. "Maybe the junk distracted the sharks. I don't know. Whatever the reason, they didn't attack me.

"One of the pirates, he leaned over the rail of the boat to get a good view of me and the sharks. He burst out laughing."

Liko watched her hazel eyes dart side to side as she reran the memory.

"I meant nothing to him. I meant less to him than the empty baskets floating around me. He didn't even wait to see if the sharks attacked me. He was totally indifferent. He turned his back to me and walked away."

"If I had been there I would have helped you," Liko said.

Toi focused on Liko's face, studying him for a moment. "Yes, I believe you would have tried. And the pirates would have killed you. They would have killed you for sure."

"Maybe," Liko said. "Maybe not."

They sat for a while, seated next to each other, watching the sharks. Liko felt Toi's body heat and could smell her body's perfume. He wanted to reach out and wipe away a bead of perspiration that slowly crossed her forehead, then descended in front of her ear and down her neck. But the moment passed and Toi wiped it with her sleeve.

They got up after a while and strolled from one exhibit to another until they stood in front of a tank containing an orange anemone fish, guarding its eggs. "It starts out one sex and then changes to another," Toi said.

Liko was astounded. "It's protandrous?"

"Yeah." She looked at him and laughed. "How in the world did you know that?"

"A friend told me. She told me all about the parrotfish too, how they start out one sex and then change to another."

"I'm impressed."

"I saw a parrotfish during my night dive last year. It had sealed itself in a cocoon and was asleep." He didn't tell her that a diver had speared it.

"I brought my dive gear," he added.

They left the aquarium and strolled to San Souci. They watched the sun set from the bench overlooking the beach where they had first met almost a year ago. After that, they strolled down Kalakaua Avenue, beneath the ironwood trees, to where Toi had parked in front of the aquarium.

Liko wanted to kiss her, but instead he nervously asked, "Let's dive this weekend."

"I'd like that," she said.

CHAPTER
SIX

"You're a reef wrecker!" Toi yelled at Liko as they surfaced just short of a sandy beach in water shallow enough for them to stand up in. She removed her scuba mask and let it dangle around her neck. "I have never seen anyone damage so much so quickly. What's the matter with you?"

"What?" Liko was shocked. "What did I do?"

"You're destroying the reef!"

"No I'm not."

"You kicked the coral. You stood on the ocean floor. You were crushing small invertebrates and destroying their burrows." She paused to catch her breath. "And how dare you bully that octopus!"

"The bubbles didn't hurt it," Liko said, surprised that she was upset. "All I did was flush it out of the *puka*. What's wrong with that?" He had stuck his alternate regulator into a crevice in the coral and had blasted the octopus with compressed air. So what?

Toi stared at him with a look of disgust. "It's callous."

Perhaps she was right—right about his diving skills, not the octopus. His diving skills were horrendous. During his junior year he had improved his swimming, but not his diving. *I am a terrible diver*, he admitted to himself.

But he hadn't hurt the octopus, he'd just gotten a better view. And that's why he had chased the parrotfish, too. It fascinated him: its multi-colored body was beautiful, its life cycle, incredible.

Toi waded ashore—Liko had to crawl on all fours because he kept tripping on his dive fins and falling down—and then, in silence, they carried their dive gear to her Honda hatchback. They loaded the heavy scuba tanks first. Then Toi used their jackets and fins and booties to wedge the tanks so they wouldn't roll around. And then they threw their masks and snorkels on top.

As Toi drove her little blue car along the beach road back towards Waikiki, neither said a word.

Liko was wishing that he could redo the dive, follow her lead, be more careful. She was an excellent diver. He should have watched her, learned from her. Instead, he had struck out on his own. And instead of impressing her, he had disappointed her. *I'm an idiot*, he thought, angry at himself.

After a few miles, Toi detoured and sped down several side streets and parked the car parallel to a narrow beach.

She turned to him and said in an angry tone of voice, "If we're going to dive together, you're going to learn buoyancy control."

A wave of embarrassment washed over him. Her anger was so disconcerting that he dropped all thoughts of defending himself, or looking good, or impressing her.

"Are you willing to learn?"

"Yes."

"Okay then, we can practice here. It's flat and muddy—a good place to learn balance and buoyancy."

They soon had their gear on and were trudging to the water's edge in their black booties. When they reached the high-water line, Toi turned and said, "I'll go first, show you how to do it, then you follow me." She stepped backwards into the mud and her feet sank. With each difficult step there was a sucking noise.

Nevertheless, she walked slowly and gracefully across the mudflat until the water was waist deep and she was twenty yards from the beach. Then she leaned back into the water and floated on her back. She pulled on her fins, popped in her snorkel, and rolled over onto her stomach—completing a smooth, perfect entry.

Liko observed her effortless grace as she reversed her demonstration: She rolled onto her back, took off her fins, stood up, and pushed the mask onto her forehead.

She yelled at him across the mudflat. "If you learn how to walk in this shit—" she paused for effect, "you won't have to crawl on your hands and knees."

The admonishment stung.

He strode into the muck.

"No! No! Turn around and walk in backwards," she ordered. "Take smaller steps."

Liko had no desire to walk across twenty yards of mudflats; however, he knew that a refusal would end their relationship.

"I'm coming," he mumbled. He turned around and stepped backwards into the mud. His bootie sank into the ooze. He pulled his foot out and black mud flowed off like molasses. It was disgusting.

He shuffled slowly backwards, pulling up brown goo. Soon, a large mud cloud surrounded his knees.

He cussed under his breath.

He lost his balance and fell sideways and his head plunged below the surface.

The poor visibility reminded him of his quarry dive—a much worse disaster. His mood changed instantly, and he asked himself, *Is this as far as I've come?*

He had learned to swim. He had lifted weights and had lost body fat. He had felt prepared for anything. But now, after only one fall, he again felt like his former self: clumsy and fat and embarrassed. He hated his Koholua genes.

He let go of his fins and tried to push off the muddy ocean floor with his hands but instead of rising, he sank. The mud oozed between his fingers and up his forearms to his elbows. It was revolting.

He rolled sideways and then struggled to his knees. He sank into the ooze. His hands up to his elbows, his legs, and the left side of his body were now streaked with black mud. He pulled up his regulator and second stage; both were encased in globs of mud. He searched for his fins and found them in the mud. He scooped a handful of mud out of the pocket of his new buoyancy control jacket his great-aunt had given him last summer. It was all muddy.

His embarrassment turned to humiliation.

He struggled to his feet and again started walking backwards through the mudflat towards Toi, pulling one foot loose and then the other. And then his hands were grasping the air for something to hold onto but there was nothing, and he heard his own pathetic cry as he fell back into the muddy water and went under the surface again.

He again stood up. Again found the fins.

"Please help me! Help me?"

Toi negotiated the mudflats to stand at his side. In a matter-of-fact tone of voice she had him remove his jacket and tank. Then they washed off the mud, together.

After that Toi ordered him back to the beach. When he reached the beach, she instructed him to practice his entrance again. He wasn't used to taking orders, but he obeyed.

After several more dunkings, he slowly discovered his balance. He also learned to pull his fins on while in the water.

Then she taught him buoyancy control. At first his fins kicked up mud, but soon he learned to control himself, and before long he was able to float six to twelve inches above the muddy ocean floor without touching it, his body slowing rising then descending with each shallow breath.

He hoped that her mood was changing and that he was working his way back into her favor. This humiliation—floating face down, his nose six inches from black, oozy mud—was a small price to pay. He had cheated on his scuba skills in the quarry, holding the wooden platform and performing pushups instead of fin pivots. But now, under Toi's guidance, he finally mastered buoyancy control. She made him float at different depths for almost an hour, until he was cold and exhausted and had used up all the air in his tank. But he mastered the skill.

"Let's go home," Toi said, all of the anger gone from her voice.

In response, Liko stood up and, for the fun of it, let his fins sink into the mud again under the weight of his massive body. Then he reached into the black gunk and took them off, using the quick release mechanism. He pulled a fin to the surface and stood there looking at the black ooze dripping from it. Smiling. Inexplicably happy!

To his surprise, Toi took the fin from him and slowly poured out the remaining mud as if she was looking for something of value.

When she didn't find anything, she asked for his other fin, which he gave to her, gladly. Again she sifted through the mud, looking for something.

"Amphioxus," Toi said. "It's a small, segmented worm."

"You mean something lives in this shit?"

"Life is amazingly adaptive," Toi answered. "*Pikaia gracilens* was alive and swimming and foraging in fertile mud like this a half billion years ago, during the Cambrian explosion."

"During the time of the dinosaurs?"

"Long before the dinosaurs. *Gracilens* was the first known chordate. The father of all vertebrates."

"You lost me," Liko said.

"That means it was the common ancestor of all animals with backbones, not only the dinosaurs but also you and me."

"You telling me I'm descended from some worm that lived in mud?"

"It was a worm with a solid, cartilaginous rod—the notochord—that ran down its back."

"I thought we descended from monkeys, not worms," Liko joked, chuckling.

Toi looked at him. His chuckle reminded her of his Uncle Keahi. "Our origins are very humble, Liko. Pikaia's offspring survived to evolve into *Homo sapiens*, but it didn't have to be that way. *That* is why it is so humbling. Any one of the hundreds of other creatures that lived during the time of Pikaia could have survived instead, and life would have evolved in a totally different direction. Had that happened, there may never have been *any* creatures with backbones, like you and me. That is what is so humbling."

"What did this Pikaia look like?"

"It was a swimmer," Toi said. "It had a pointed, cobra-like flat head. And a tail something like a snail's tail."

"Head of a cobra and tail of a snail?"

They locked arms as they walked ashore, balancing each other.

The next day, Toi took Liko to her favorite dive spot, off the Toilet Bowl. When they arrived at Hanauma Bay, the trade winds were blowing but the waves were small.

In light wetsuits and full gear, they executed a beach entry as smoothly as two monk seals sliding into the ocean. Then they snorkeled out of the protected snorkel area, through the reef, across the area where Liko and Angelica had almost drowned the previous summer, and then to Toilet Bowl Point.

Once they reached the wall of the crater, near the inlet to the toilet bowl, Toi gave instructions. "Our dive plan is to scuba clockwise, following the outer edge of the finger coral, fifty to eighty feet below the surface. When we reach the opposite wall of the bay"—she pointed to the far wall—"there, just south of Witches Brew, we will explore the boulders for 15 minutes. The boulders are twenty to thirty feet below the surface. From there we will continue clockwise to the undersea telephone cables in the center of the bay. We will then surface and follow the cables back through the slot to the beach. Any questions?"

It was a simple, circular dive plan in moderately deep water. "No, let's do it."

They descended effortlessly and then Liko followed Toi on her left, just behind her shoulder. When they reached the submerged outer reef, he adjusted his buoyancy control. It worked. He felt immensely pleased with himself. They floated sixty feet below the surface, allowing the surge to move their bodies slowly back and forth, hovering together.

Gravity was pulling them downward, yet they floated with perfect buoyancy control. They drifted sideways, as if the ocean willed their bodies to move. Then a swell pushed them back to their starting point, as if the ocean had had second thoughts. They stayed together, floated and drifted together.

A school of large mullet approached, their dual dorsal fins erect, their bodies silver and fast. The mullet divided and swam around them, then disappeared into deeper water.

Liko thought he heard a whisper. He looked but saw only coral on calcareous, skeletal rock.

He sensed something: the sand on the ocean floor? The coral? The water? The fish? It all seemed to be alive. The entire ocean seemed suddenly alive.

The cool water whispered.

He checked his position in the water column: he was floating gracefully above the finger coral, maintaining his buoyancy control. He watched Toi. Her position changed slightly as she breathed slowly and her bubbles ascended, but she also maintained control, perfectly.

He felt something unseen, beyond his senses.

He thought: *This is life. The will of life.*

The feeling grew inside him. The surge, the sand, the living coral, the cool water—all had the will of life. And he knew that he was alive. And it was like a vision: a sudden, unsought, unwilled, vision of life. Of his own life. Of Toi's life. And of the living ocean.

And then something dark inside his mind fell away and was replaced with light. It was as if his eyes suddenly opened, and he could see everything clearly.

He felt ecstatic.

He took Toi's hand and led her in an underwater waltz, and they whirled in the water column.

Everything was precious. Nothing was fragile. Happiness enveloped him and glowed warm and bright inside his body and mind.

Later, after they surfaced near the slot, he tried to express these thoughts and feelings to Toi.

She listened carefully, concern filling her eyes. After he finished, she commented: "You were narked."

"Narked?"

"Yeah, narked." She shook her head. "I'm surprised that it happened at sixty feet. Usually it happens at a hundred feet or deeper."

"What happens?"

"You felt euphoric?"

"I did, yes."

"Everything melted away?"

"Oh, yes!"

She frowned. "Tell me, did you want to stay under, not surface?"

"I did, yes." He slowly nodded his head. *I felt like I could take off my mask and breathe the water. I felt invincible.* Now he began to understand what she was telling him. "I felt a part of everything, as if I was one with everything. As if everything was alive, even the sand, the coral, the water. As if I had discovered a kinship, a forgotten relationship. And you are right; I wanted to stay, not leave. I felt fantastic, happy, alive, as if I had found my place in the universe."

Toi looked at him, a troubled expression on her face. "Getting narked at sixty to seventy feet—such a shallow depth—is not a good thing."

His gaze swept the surface of the ocean.

"Liko, the ocean is unforgiving."

Maybe narked, maybe not. Nevertheless, he knew that the experience had changed him. He was now eager to dive back in, to return to the mother of all life, the ocean.

CHAPTER
SEVEN

Keahi stepped out of his apartment grounds onto the sidewalk along Pualei Circle. He was dressed casually in a pair of khaki shorts, a muted aloha shirt, and comfortable slippers. A heavy gold chain hung around his suntanned neck. He carried three grass mats, rolled up, in the crook of his arm—one for himself, one for Carol, and one for Angelica. They were his two best friends and religiously lifted weights with him at the gym in Waikiki.

All day he had looked forward to the evening's benefit concert at the aquarium; the Makiki Sons, traditional Hawaiian musicians, were performing. Their voices were majestic, their harmonies beautiful.

It was less than half a mile to the aquarium, so he walked. He always walked if his destination was in the shadow of either Diamond Head or the hotels in Waikiki.

When he reached the entrance to Pualei Circle, he crossed Leahi Street and cut through a community garden, where he stopped long enough to admire the colorful flowers and ripe vegetables growing in four-by-eight-foot raised beds, and to inhale the rich earthy smell of compost and fresh chicken manure. Leaving the garden, he crossed Paki Street, negotiating heavy traffic. Then he crossed a wide concrete jogging path and walked onto the grassy, huge central lawn of Kapiolani Park. He was now inside the jogging path that looped two miles around the park and enclosed soccer and softball and rugby fields.

At the moment though, the park was quiet. Very quiet. It was late and all the children and their parents had gone home.

Dry, downtrodden grass rubbed against the sides of his feet as he walked across the chalked outline of an empty soccer field. He avoided several bare patches of red earth, where the field was overused and the grass had died.

Then he passed along the back side of the Waikiki Shell.

Keahi, Angelica and Carol had listened to many concerts in this grassy area. Many times they had set up folding chairs, a Smokey Joe, and a small Coleman cooler filled with food and beer. With other locals, they had barbecued and talked story and listened to the concerts for free.

Keahi had spent many evenings here with Daniel, too. He recalled lying on his back in the grass, his head cradled in Daniel's lap. Together they had watched the stars twinkle in a black velvety sky as Van Cliburn played Chopin's *Scherzo in C-sharp minor*, Beethoven's *Appassionata*, Debussy's *Reflets dans l'eau* and *L'Isle joyeuse*.

He felt a quick rush of grief.

"Daniel was my center," he whispered to himself. "Without him, I have no guiding star."

The cool trade winds blew in his face and he looked ahead and saw clouds through the ironwood trees on the far side of the park. The clouds hung over the ocean, near the horizon, waiting to bid the sun farewell.

He continued across the worn-out soccer fields and past the tennis courts. There he crossed the concrete jogging path again, and then negotiated his way through bumper-to-bumper cars on both sides of the median strip on Kalakaua Avenue. After that, he passed under the first of two rows of majestic ironwood trees.

He turned left and strolled down the sidewalk, flanked on each side by the tall ironwoods, stopping occasionally to remove bristly brown cones from between his slippers and bare feet. They hurt. The cones were the size of acorns and on close examination they looked like tiny, prickly hedgehogs.

When he finally arrived at the Waikiki Aquarium, he found Carol and Angelica patiently waiting for him outside. They were also dressed casually in Bermuda shorts and T-shirts and slippers. An elderly volunteer at the front entrance took their tickets and they passed through the aquarium lobby to an outdoor area in the back of the building, across from the monk seal tank.

It was a beautiful night for a concert: the trade winds were blowing and it was cool. The sun would soon light up the clouds and set into the ocean. There were no mosquitoes.

They wandered through the enthusiastic, congenial crowd until they came to an open-air stage. There Keahi unrolled the three grass mats onto the lush grass in front of the small wooden stage. He checked twice to make sure he was a comfortable distance from the large, black speakers, which were raised on tripods on both sides of the stage.

The Makiki Sons had not yet arrived, so Keahi, Carol and Angelica sat on the mats and talked story and watched families spread out their picnic blankets, take off their slippers or shoes, and relax. Everyone was dressed casually except for a few older women who were dressed in tastefully colorful *muumuus*. The older women sat in a row of folding chairs to one side of the low stage.

Parents seemed oblivious to the ruckus raised by their *keiki*, who ran among family members and strangers alike as if everyone at the concert was part of one large, extended family. *Keiki* ran wildly on the green lawn, happy to be outdoors and carefree. They danced on the lawn like the pollen from the ironwood trees blowing in the air.

It was a happy, enthusiastic, relaxed audience of one hundred or so people. The lawn overflowed with loud conversations and laughter. It reminded Keahi of a big family *luau*.

"Are you guys hungry? Thirsty?" he asked Carol and Angelica. "I'm going for hamburgers and Cokes. Would you like something?"

"A hamburger," Carol said. "Loaded with everything. And a package of chips. And a Diet Coke."

"I'll have the same," Angelica said, "but no onions on mine. Hey, I'll go with you and help you carry everything."

Keahi glanced at Carol who said, "Go ahead. I'll people-watch."

So Angelica got up and helped Keahi to his feet. They carefully picked their way through the seated crowd to the edge of the lawn, where they joined a long line that wound along the perimeter fence on the ocean side, and eventually wound its way to a grill where volunteers were charbroiling hamburgers.

While waiting, Keahi looked to his left through the perimeter fence and out to the setting sun. Hovering half its width above the ocean, the sun was a bright orange ball, and sunrays were skipping off the water, sparkling.

A large group had gathered just outside the chain link fence to listen to the concert for free, just like Keahi often did behind the Waikiki Shell. Silhouetted in the sunlight were two figures sitting side by side with their backs to Keahi and their feet dangling over the concrete shore wall. The setting sun and the ocean and rays of brilliant light framed them.

Then Keahi recognized one of the two silhouetted figures: It was Toi. At first he was surprised but then he recalled that she volunteered part-time at the aquarium. He wondered if she had helped with the concert tonight, too.

He watched as the other silhouetted figure—a young man – bumped shoulders with her, affectionately. And then the sun touched the ocean and Keahi knew that the fiery ball would slip away in seconds. The scene was as picturesque as a local postcard.

Toi and the man were laughing. Keahi could not hear their laughter, but he could hear the waves slapping against the seawall and he wondered if the salt spray was wetting their feet.

He thought it was nice that Toi had a boyfriend. He missed Daniel and remembered a time when he and Daniel had also sat together on the wall, not far from where Toi and her friend were now sitting.

Then the young man turned to face Toi and Keahi recognized his profile. It was Liko!

Keahi stood bewildered, gazing through the fence, trying to understand what he was seeing. He was dumbfounded.

He watched as they laughed and he grew even more confused. He recognized the family chuckle, faint but distinct. Why hadn't Toi told him about Liko? Didn't she know that Liko was his nephew? And why hadn't Liko said something?

A torrent of questions flooded his mind. Was Toi the girl Liko had called last summer on his last day in Hawaii before he returned to Nevada? Was Toi the girl Liko had written to during his junior year? Was Toi the girl he was dating?

He felt betrayed and hurt. *Why didn't they say something to me!*

Then Toi turned and saw Keahi and her carefree smile changed to an expression of sharp surprise and at the same time the sun dropped into the ocean. She nudged Liko and said something to him and he wheeled around. His searching eyes met Keahi's puzzled expression.

The pink sky between the clouds seemed to stretch thin like a taunt balloon, ready to burst at any moment.

Keahi turned away and exhaled deeply.

"What's wrong?" Angelica asked.

He didn't answer.

"Are you okay?" Angelica looked at Keahi carefully. "Why so glum all of a sudden?"

She looked around trying to discover what had upset him. Then she spotted Liko. "Hey! Isn't that Liko?" She waved and he waved back. "And who is that great looking girl with him?"

"Great looking girl?" Keahi fought to control himself. "She's a friend from work. Her name's Toi."

"You must introduce me." Angelica waved at Toi and Toi waved back, a smile returning to her face.

"She's cute. Looks like Liko found himself a cute one."

"She is old enough to be his mother!" Keahi countered.

"What a fuddy-duddy!"

"What?"

"You heard me," Angelica said.

Keahi frowned: Angelica was much too delighted.

"You know," Angelica said, "last summer Liko had a crush on me and I was afraid it would end badly. But now he's found a girlfriend. That's good—very good!"

"The last thing he needs is encouragement," Keahi said, annoyed.

The line crawled, but they eventually got their food and returned to Carol, who was chatting with neighbors on adjoining grass mats.

After they sat down and the concert started, Angelica whispered in Keahi's ear, "Didn't they look great together, though!"

Keahi sat on the grass mat with his legs crossed. He felt hurt and small.

The Makiki Sons played—two guitars, an upright bass, and their majestic voices. After a few verses, Keahi abandoned himself to their harmonies. But all too soon the song ended and he returned to the real world and remembered the sunset silhouette. He wanted to whirl around and see if Liko and Toi were still there, but he kept his back to the ocean.

After the Makiki Sons performed their last encore and the crowd stopped their enthusiastic applause, and after saying a quick goodnight to Angelica and Carol, Keahi went around to the seawall. But Liko and Toi had left.

Ten minutes later he was in his studio, where he was shocked to find them waiting on his lanai, seated together on his gliding love seat.

"Hello," Liko said, awkwardly.

Keahi returned the greeting and sat down in a chair at the glass table, within arm's reach of Toi. He noticed that Liko's arm rested across the back of the loveseat behind Toi's head. All three faced away from the studio and into the night sky.

Toi appeared nervous. Liko, on the other hand, seemed cheerful and upbeat. And Keahi? Well, he felt awkward. He was upset, and also unsure what his role should be. Should he act the part of co-worker? Friend? Parent?

There was an uncomfortable moment of silence, and then they talked about the weather and the night sky. After that the silence returned.

As Keahi struggled to find something to say, it dawned on him that he knew nothing about Toi's family. He had worked with her for years, yet he knew very little about her, and nothing about her family. It seemed like a safe subject: family history, perhaps dull, but safe—like talking about the weather. So he ventured a question: "Toi, do you have any brothers?"

"No, I don't have any brothers or sisters."

"Are your parents here, in Hawaii?"

"No, my mother died." Toi looked at him inquiringly. "I don't know where my father is."

"Oh," he said. "I'm sorry to hear that."

"It's okay," she said. "I never knew him. He was a soldier. My mother met him in Vietnam, and he returned to the States before Saigon fell."

"So you came here when you were a kid?"

"No. The postwar mood was not sympathetic to children like me. Americans didn't want us. We were a constant reminder that they had lost the war."

When Keahi said nothing, Toi continued. "When I was older, they passed the Amerasian Act. It granted admission privileges."

"So is that when you came to Hawaii?"

"No. The United States welcomed me, but excluded my mother. She couldn't come with me." Toi paused, remembering. "My mother was told to sign an irrevocable release giving up custody of me, but she refused. How could she let me go? How could she turn me over to strangers in a foreign country?"

"Didn't your father help?" Liko asked, joining the conversation.

"After my father left Vietnam, my mother lost touch with him. I don't know where he is, or even if he is still alive." Toi looked down at her small feet, a sad expression on her face. "When I was young I used to have a dream of traveling to America. And in my dream my father always met me when I arrived."

"I believe that my mother made the right decision, though. She kept me with her and we stayed in Vietnam. We stayed together and that seems right."

"So how did you get here?" Liko asked. "How did you get to America?"

Toi smiled at him. "I came after I lost my mother. I made the journey with several hundred boat people. First to Thailand, eventually to America."

Keahi felt deeply embarrassed. What had started as a simple question about family had elicited very personal memories.

"Hawaii must have been very different after growing up in Vietnam?" Liko asked.

"Yes, it was. I have a lot of good memories, a few bad ones, and some funny ones."

"Tell us a funny one," Liko requested, smiling.

"Before I came to America, I had never had a Whopper. Can you imagine that?"

Liko shook his head, no.

"I was very young and I'd never had a Whopper. But I had seen billboard advertisements for Burger King. So I marched proudly into a local Burger King and asked for a 'Burger King.' Everyone laughed at me. I will never forget that. I insisted I wanted a 'Burger King!' The more I insisted, the more they laughed. I finally got the Whopper, but it wasn't until later that I understood why they were laughing. It is funny now, but at the time it devastated me."

Keahi looked at Liko, who was smiling at Toi affectionately.

"I had problems in school, too," Toi continued. "My mother had taught me English, but with a Vietnamese accent."

Yes, even today you sing your words, Keahi thought.

"And to make matters worse, the local kids shunned me. I quickly learned that correct English was only for school. Outside, all the kids spoke pidgin. If I spoke proper English the kids picked on me, knocked my books out of my hands, and laughed at me—stuff like that."

Toi reflected for a few moments then added, "The first after-school job I had was at a pet shop. Even then I knew that I wanted to dive and explore the ocean. So I saved my money and bought snorkeling gear. Then I enrolled in a scuba class."

"That reminds me," Liko said, "I want to tell you guys something."

"What?" Keahi asked.

"I'm going cave diving!"

Keahi saw alarm on Toi's face and concern in her eyes.

"A guy at the dive shop invited me to go cave diving," Liko said. "Isn't that great?"

"What?" Toi said. Keahi could hear the concern in her voice.

"The guy at the dive shop, the guy who fills my tanks, he asked if I wanted to dive the lava tubes and I said yes."

"Which tube dive?" Keahi asked.

"Off Shark's Cove."

"The Elevator Shaft?"

"Yeah," Liko said, "I think that's what he called it."

"Do you know that three Marines died there?" Toi asked.

"Three Marines?"

"Yes, from Kaneohe Marine Corps Base."

"What happened?"

"They were diving the caves and the ocean surge stirred up the sand, clouded everything. They probably got disoriented and ran out of air. Their bodies were found inside the Elevator Shaft."

"In the caves off Pupukea Beach Park?"

"That's the area," Toi said. "You get into the caves by wading out to the Elevator Shaft. It's a maze. If you get lost, if you follow the wrong tube—you drown."

"I'll be careful."

"Careful?" Toi said. "You need training to cave dive."

"The shop guy's a good diver."

"But you're not," Toi said. "Has someone taught you to dive caves?"

"I've got to learn some time."

"The shaft is not the way to start," Toi said.

"Keahi, what do you think?" Liko asked.

"I agree with Toi," he said.

"Besides," Toi added, "the last time we went diving—at Hanauma Bay—you remember what happened?"

Liko shook his head, not wanting to answer.

"You should tell your uncle."

"What?" Keahi asked.

"He got narked." Toi said.

Surprised, Keahi focused on Liko, waiting for his response.

"It happened one time," Liko said, defending himself. He withdrew his arm from around Toi's neck.

"But it was at sixty feet, Liko!"

"I was tired," he said. "I wasn't myself that day."

Toi told Keahi all about Liko getting narked.

After that, Keahi stared thoughtfully at Liko, then decided, "You don't have my permission to go cave diving."

"What am I supposed to tell the guy?" he angrily asked, raising his voice. "He needs a dive buddy."

Toi and Keahi looked at each other and shook their heads in amazement.

"Do you have the training to help him if he gets into trouble?" Toi asked.

"If your friend knew what he was doing," Keahi added, "he wouldn't have chosen you for a dive partner."

Liko sat still, his arms now folded across his chest. He was bristling with indignation.

He looked at Toi and for the first time was aware of their age difference. She should have sided with him. Instead, she was treating him like a kid.

CHAPTER EIGHT

IT WAS MIDMORNING AND LIKO WAS ON Jack's roof helping him nail shingles. The early morning had been cool, with a northeasterly breeze, but now the sun was higher in the sky and the air had warmed up, so Liko pulled off his T-shirt and let the sun warm his broad shoulders. He handed Jack another shingle. Jack carefully aligned it along a white chalk line on the black roofing paper and then nailed it into place.

The work was tedious but easier than stripping off layers of crumbly old shingles and replacing rotten plywood sheeting, which Liko had done last week. Fortunately the roof was a simple hip frame, so the work was uncomplicated and required little skill. Liko was grateful that Keahi had found him the job.

But what a job! Especially for an old man like Jack! Why was he replacing the roof himself? Why didn't he hire a roofing company? *He's an old guy*, Liko thought, *too old to be up here.*

In fact, Liko was so concerned about Jack's age and health that he always got to work early, before Jack had the chance to begin without him. Indeed, Liko was afraid to arrive late. What if Jack fell off the ladder? What if he overexerted himself because Liko wasn't there to help and he suffered a heart attack? Or a stroke? Along with these worries, Liko's feeling of responsibility grew daily; he didn't want to oversleep or show up late for work.

Besides, Liko enjoyed the work. He knew that carrying the shingles up the ladder was good exercise, even if it did send his calves into spasms of fire. And as an extra benefit, he now had a deep tan.

"Something on your mind?" Jack asked.

"Yes."

After starting with that simple admission, Liko surprised himself and opened up, telling Jack all about his relationship with Toi. How they had met at San Souci. How she had taught him buoyancy control in the mudflats. How Keahi had discovered their relationship during the Makiki Sons benefit concert. He told Jack about his argument with Toi and Keahi concerning the cave dive.

"They are right, you know." Jack handed Liko another shingle. "You would be smart to listen and obey."

"Well, it's my decision isn't it? Toi should have supported me," he added, "instead, she took Keahi's side."

"Unremitting embarrassment," Jack posited. "Is that the way you see it?"

How did he know? Liko stared at Jack, amazed at his insight. *Just by climbing the ladder and sitting on the roof with me, enjoying the sun and the fresh air and the view, occasionally handing me a shingle, he's gotten me to work twice as hard as I normally would.* Liko chuckled. *And I'm enjoying it.*

Later, around ten o'clock, just after he had carried a heavy package of shingles up the ladder, Liko stood up straight and stretched out the knotting muscles in his back. That's when he saw an old Japanese man walking down the road with a small boy, about four years old. They were carrying bamboo fishing poles and the Japanese man had a wicker basket.

Liko watched them as they turned off the road and sauntered down Jack's driveway to a small, yellow-brown cottage adjacent to Jack's beach house. Liko and Jack, from their vantage point on the roof, could see into both backyards.

The Japanese man stopped at the back of the cottage, where he inverted the wicker basket and shook it. Something snakelike and glistening fell out onto the grass.

"Looks like he caught a *puhi*," Jack said.

"Do people eat those things?"

"He must think that it's *ono*, good. Myself, I think eels are repulsive."

"Have you eaten one?"

"Nope," Jack said. "And I never will. And I don't eat seaweed or sea urchins either."

As they talked, the old man set the eel on a wide, weathered board that lay on the grass. He knelt beside it and the little boy stood next to him, watching.

The first cut was behind the gills. Then, starting at the gills, the old man slit the eel all the way down the belly. With his fingers he pulled out the shiny intestines. Next, he returned to the head and cut through the backbone to the skin on the opposite side of the body. Then he picked up the eel. Liko could see that the head was still attached to the body by a thick layer of skin. The old man grasped the head and, using it for leverage, he began pulling the skin away from the body. Occasionally the skin wouldn't separate from the flesh, and the old man would stop his tugging, set the eel down on the board, and cut the recalcitrant flesh away from the skin. The old man discarded the skin in a black plastic bag, along with the eel's head. Next he cut off the tail and removed the fins. And then the old man rinsed the eel under the outdoor faucet at the back of the cottage. As he rinsed out the belly, he ran his fingers thoroughly over the flesh until he seemed satisfied it was clean. He handed the eel to the small boy who held it at arm's length, the white flesh almost touching the ground. The old fisherman rinsed his hands and then led the boy—still holding the eel—into the cottage.

"I could use something cold to drink," Jack said to Liko. "How about you?"

"Sounds good. That was like watching the Discovery Channel."

They climbed down the ladder.

"Do you own that little cottage?"

"No," Jack replied. "Well, not yet anyway. When my mother passed away she left me this beach house and that guest cottage. But she made a provision in her will that allows that old fisherman to live next door until he passes away. Then the cottage becomes mine. In the meantime, though, he lives there for free. But I have to pay the taxes!"

"Why did she do that?" Liko was curious. It was an unusual and very generous arrangement.

"I don't know. But he's been here a long time. The executor said the old man was living here when my mother bought the place, and that was a long, long time ago, before my stepfather died."

"Does the boy live here, too?"

"The boy's father died in a head-on car crash on the Big Island. I don't know about his mother. To be honest, I am little interested in the old man or the boy."

"I've heard that the roads on the Big Island are terrible," Liko said, trying to build on the conversation. "Seems like there are a lot of bad accidents over there."

Jack, however, didn't comment on the roads, nor did he provide details about the crash. In fact, he became very quiet.

Eventually Liko brought the conversation back around to the old fisherman. "Do you mind him living next door?"

"Mind? Why?"

Liko shrugged. Jack's cottage was isolated, yet he had little privacy because his neighbor was literally on the same lot.

"I'm not happy about the arrangement," Jack said, "if that's what you're asking."

Liko worked hard on Sunday and Monday, putting in two full days from sunrise to sunset. Jack had been anxious to get the roof finished, even though it seldom rained on the leeward side of the island and storms were not forecast for the rest of the week. On Tuesday he arrived for work early, yet he found Jack already up on the roof, nailing shingles.

He's too old to work this hard, Liko thought as he climbed to the top of the ladder and stepped onto the roof.

Jack greeted him gruffly. "Why did you leave that rock on my doorstep? I could have broken my neck."

"What rock?"

"The rock by my front door."

Liko grabbed a shingle and handed it to Jack. "I have no idea what you're talking about."

Jack looked at him with a puzzled expression. "If it wasn't you, then who put it there?"

Liko shrugged his shoulders. How was he supposed to know?

Jack considered that for a moment, then turned his attention to the shingle. He aligned it with the chalk line and nailed it to the roof.

They didn't talk about the rock again until their mid-morning break, when they climbed down from the roof and Jack showed him the rock. It was eight inches in diameter and covered with lichen that was brown with white mottling and flecks of yellow.

"I've never seen that rock before," Liko said. "The lichen is remarkable, though."

"What?"

"The lichen—it's the underbelly of the biosphere. I studied it in my biology class. Given enough time, that lichen will break down that rock."

"Great," Jack said, jokingly. "A big rock carrying a unique life form shows up on my doorstep and I almost break my neck. It must have been placed there by an alien."

Liko stepped to the edge of the porch. He took a long drink of water from a plastic squeeze bottle as he surveyed the wild vegetation that grew right up to the porch.

"Hey, guess what I see?" he said, surprise in his voice. His eyes had picked out a shape among the overgrown ginger, not far from the foot of the ladder that was leaning against the side of the house. He climbed over the porch railing and carefully lowered himself down into the ginger.

"That's our next project," Jack said. "I need to thin the ginger."

Liko pushed the ginger aside and picked up a large rock, which he then placed on top of the railing. Soon more rocks were lined up on the railing, like turtles on a log.

"My God!" Jack said, watching in amazement. "It must be the *menehunes*!"

"*Menehunes*?" Liko asked, climbing back onto the porch.

"Yes—you know, the little people."

"You mean the kid next door?"

An expression of surprise filled Jack's face. "Maybe so." He pursed his lips and nodded his head. "The rocks are large, yet not too large for a kid to move around. *Menehunes* were dwarfs. According to Hawaiian legend, *menehune* gathered rocks and built the heiau—the temples—and fishponds."

"But why? Why would the kid do something like this?"

"Kids are uncivilized animals," Jack stated, matter-of-factly.

Liko waited for Jack to explain.

"They live in the present. They do what they want. They're self-centered, wild animals."

Jack picked up two rocks and knocked them together. "I should talk to his grandfather."

"I'm sure the kid meant no harm."

"Really? I could have broken my neck."

After Jack finished his soda, they climbed back up onto the roof and nailed more shingles. And so the morning passed, and so did lunch. Late afternoon found Liko still hammering while Jack talked story.

Just before sunset they spotted the boy coming down the driveway. He had a stick in his hand and he was whacking everything within reach: the mock orange hedge along the edge of the driveway, the white plumeria blossoms on low-hanging branches, and the deep red hibiscus flowers that grew between Jack's beach house and the old fisherman's cottage. Severed flower heads, red and white, sailed through the air and dropped to the gravel.

"Stop that!" Jack yelled, setting his hammer down on the roofing paper and scrambling across the roof to the ladder. He climbed down so fast that Liko thought he was falling.

The boy froze and looked up at Jack with fright in his wide eyes. His mouth contorted.

"Did you put a rock by my door?" Jack demanded as he stepped off the bottom rung and swung around to face the boy. "Answer me!"

The boy's head moved slowly up and down, signaling a clear, frightened yes.

"I could have broken my neck!"

Jack closed in on the boy, who burst into a loud wail and started bawling.

"Now, none of that!"

The boy tried to stop crying. He gulped air a few times, let out a couple of uncontrollable sobs, and then started sniffling. His nose started to run.

"I won't have any crying, or whacking my bushes, or putting rocks around my yard. Understand?"

The boy was shaking in his slippers as Jack stood over him.

That was too much for Liko. He climbed down the ladder and quickly covered the ground to the boy and Jack. "Let me talk to him," Liko interjected, stepping in between the two of them. He knelt so he was eye to eye with the boy. Tears were flowing and snot was running from his nose.

"It's going to be all right," Liko said in a soft voice. "He's just upset because he tripped on one of your rocks." He paused and smiled. "Listen, I'll help you carry them back home, okay?"

"No!" Jack interjected. "That's not okay."

"I don't mind moving them," Liko said.

"Thanks, but—"

Liko rubbed the boy's hair. "Go on home now."

The boy wiped his nose with the back of his hand, sniffled, then said timidly to Liko, "The rocks keep her away."

"Keep who away?" Liko asked.

"When it's dark," the boy whispered. "To take me away."

The boy's eyes again conveyed fear, and now his breathing was short and quick.

Liko glanced at Jack. A sudden, troubled expression had spread across Jack's face, too.

"What does she look like?" Jack asked. Liko thought Jack's voice sounded dry, like he had lost his spit.

"Not much clothes."

Liko glanced at Jack again; Jack's troubled expression had turned thoughtful. *What's the matter with him?* Liko wondered.

Jack reached down and grasped the boy firmly by the shoulders. "Tell your grandfather I will visit him tonight. You understand?"

Again the boy started crying.

"Good God!" Jack said, letting go of the boy so abruptly that the child fell to the ground and dropped his stick.

Liko reached out and helped the boy to his feet. He smiled lightly at the boy. Then Liko turned him around, so he was facing the cottage, and patted him gently on his bottom. "Go on home now."

The boy ran down the driveway, crying, and slipped through an opening in the hibiscus hedge between the beach house and the cottage.

"Little bugger!" Jack mumbled. "So that's how he gets through." Jack picked up the stick and pointed it at the small gap in the hedge. "He's made himself a path, a hole, in my hibiscus. Like a wild animal."

"You seemed a bit worried. You don't believe in ghosts do you?"

"Hell! I've *seen* the ghost."

"No!"

"Yes, I saw her the night I moved into the beach house." His tone was pensive, his mind, far away. "The next morning I told myself that it was the brandy, too much stress, the loss of my mother."

"And this . . . this ghost . . . 'not much clothes?'" Liko asked.

"Like the kid said, she wasn't wearing much, that's for sure. And she *was* pale. Her skin seemed translucent, otherworldly."

They thoroughly searched the yard and gathered all the rocks together into a small pile, stacking one on top of another next to the front porch stairs. They counted two dozen.

Jack picked up the lichen-covered rock again. He turned it over in his hands, feeling its weight, admiring the lichen.

"It's time I talk to the old fisherman," Jack said. "Tonight." He stared at Liko. "Will you come with me? I'd appreciate it."

The request surprised Liko and he hesitated. "I don't know." He thought about the drive from Kaena Point to Waikiki and Keahi's studio apartment — more than forty miles. "I've got a long drive."

"Liko, kids are a mystery to me. I don't know how to behave around them, and as you saw, I don't have patience with them."

Liko nodded.

"I never married and I never had kids. I think kids are wild animals. They create mayhem wherever they go. Kids need to be trained, constantly watched, continually corrected. I get along well with adults, but kids . . . I have no experience, whatsoever. And to make matters worse, I was an only child. No brothers, no sisters."

"You seem good with kids." Jack studied Liko. "And I could use your help."

Liko didn't understand.

Jack maintained eye contact. "Liko, I should be honest with you. The old fisherman, well, I've dreaded meeting him." Jack paused, almost stopped. "You see, he's the last living connection between my parents and myself. And things didn't end well between my parents and me. We argued, I left home, and we never reconciled.

"I can see by your expression that this doesn't make a lot of sense to you, but believe me, I would like you to come along. What do you say?"

He's practically begging me. A memory of the girl who had drowned in the quarry popped into Liko's mind –– front and center to his thoughts. "Yes," he mumbled to himself. "It wasn't my fault, but I could have done something."

"What?"

What if you upset the kid again? Liko thought. *How would the old fisherman react? Maybe I should be there, just in case.*

"Okay," Liko agreed. "I'll go with you. But I can't stay long. I have a long drive home and it will be dark."

It was late in the evening when Jack and Liko stopped work. They hadn't finished nailing the new shingles, but they were close. What had looked like a small job had taken twice as long as Jack had planned, but Liko wasn't surprised. After all, neither of them had roofed a house before.

As they put away the tools and washed up, Liko sensed that Jack was preoccupied. He guessed that it had something to do with the old fisherman, not the roof.

Liko was still apprehensive about tagging along. He hoped that he wouldn't be caught in the middle. He had seen arguments between neighbors in the trailer park back home turn violent. People were unpredictable, and conversations sometimes turned ugly.

"Well, I guess it's time to pay him a visit," Jack said as he dried his hands on an old T-shirt he used as a rag.

"You sure you want to? I can just throw the rocks away—easy."

"No." Jack hung the wet T-shirt on a rusty nail above the outside faucet. "It's time the old fisherman and I had a talk."

Jack went over to the pile of rocks and picked through them, turning them over, sorting them by size into three piles. He studied them, then he picked up a large, black volcanic rock.

"This one will do," he said.

Good God! Liko thought.

The old fisherman answered the door and found Jack standing in front of him with a large rock in his hand. The old fisherman smiled. "What a pleasant surprise," he said. "Please, come in." He opened his door wide.

"Did your grandson tell you that I'd be coming?"

"No," the old fisherman said. "My great-grandson said nothing. Is something wrong? Did something happen?"

Jack held out the rock.

The old fisherman's smile broadened and his face seemed to light up. He took the rock with both hands, bowed deeply and said something to Jack in Japanese. Liko wondered what all that was about.

Then the old fisherman turned the rock slowly in his hands, admiring it. *Maybe he's crazy*, Liko thought: He seemed all too pleased with the rock. Liko stole a glance at Jack and noted that he was also surprised by the old fisherman's response.

"A most interesting rock," the old fisherman said.

"Well, it's yours," Jack said.

"Thank you." He bowed deeply. "Please come in."

Jack stepped into the small cottage.

Liko thought it would be polite to introduce himself: "I'm Liko. I'm helping Jack put a new roof on his house."

The old fisherman accepted Liko's hand and warmly shook it. "Liko," he said, "I am Yukio."

"Come in, come in, Liko. Please have a seat." Yukio moved between Liko and the front door and ushered him in, and then closed the door.

A few steps later, Liko found himself standing in the middle of a small den. He waited for Jack to take a seat, and when he didn't, he remained standing.

"It's a fine new roof," Yukio said. He stepped over to a book-shelf, removed half a dozen paperback books, and set them on a lower shelf. He placed the rock in their place next to a framed photograph of a young man in a military uniform. The framed portrait was in the center of the shelf.

Liko wondered if the shelf could hold the weight.

"I almost broke my neck this morning," Jack said.

An inquiring expression filled the old fisherman's face. He turned to face Jack, tilting his head and leaning forward to catch what Jack was saying.

"Your grandson put a rock in front of my door. I tripped over it."

"I see," Yukio said.

"He put rocks all around my yard—on my front porch and in my ginger bed. And he was whacking flowers off my hibiscus."

"I see," Yukio said again, pursing his lips.

"I want it to stop."

"I see. I see." Yukio was nodding his head, now biting his lip, studying Jack. "I will remove them," he said.

"Good. They are stacked in a pile in my front yard." Jack clasped his hands. "We'll be going." He turned toward the front door.

"Please, I insist that you have a cup of tea. Please, have a seat. Make yourself comfortable. I will be back with your tea."

Before either Jack or Liko could object, the old fisherman disappeared through a door, leaving them standing. Liko looked at Jack, wondering what to do. A moment later they heard running water, and then they heard metal scraping metal; probably water had been set to boil.

"Damn," Jack muttered beneath his breath. He walked across the room and sat down on the small brown couch.

Liko walked over to the bookcase and looked at the items on the shelf. He picked up the framed photograph next to the rock and studied it. The black-and-white photo was fading. It was a young Japanese man dressed in an old-style American military uniform.

"Look at this," Liko said. He walked over to Jack and handed him the photo. Jack merely glanced at it and set it on the coffee table.

Liko sat in the chair next to Jack.

After a few quiet minutes, Yukio returned with a pot of steaming tea and sat down.

"Is that a picture of a relative?" Liko asked, motioning to the photo on the coffee table.

"That is my son, Sam," the old fisherman said. "He would be your age, Jack."

Jack picked up the framed picture again and held it in his hands. "Sam is the boy's father?" he asked.

"No," the old fisherman said. "Sam is Ned's grandfather. Ned is my great-grandson."

He opened a drawer in the center of the coffee table and lifted out a small blue box, which he held out to Jack with both hands. Jack set the framed picture back on the coffee table and accepted the small blue box.

"These were awarded to my son, Sam, for his service during World War II."

Jack opened the box. His eyes widened.

"When my son heard that the army was recruiting instructors to teach Japanese to American troops, he signed up. Sam was fluent in Japanese. The army trained him at the Military Intelligence Service language school. During the war, he translated captured Japanese war documents."

"You must be very proud of him," Jack said. Liko could tell that Jack said the words with affection.

"My son was *kibei*. He was educated in Japan. He spoke excellent Japanese."

"*Kibei?*" Liko asked.

The old fisherman explained, "Sam was born in Hawaii, but when he was two weeks old I registered him at the Japanese consulate. That way he retained his Japanese citizenship. After high school in Hawaii, he attended Waseda University in Japan and studied Japanese."

"One time, during military leave, he told me, 'Dad, I am translating battle plans.' I was very proud of him."

Jack handed the medals to Liko. "Wow! One of these is a Purple Heart." Liko said. He had never seen, much less held, a Purple Heart, but it was instantly recognizable: a bronze profile of George Washington in his Continental Army uniform, set against a purple, enameled, heart-shaped background with a bronze edge.

"Yes," the old fisherman said. "During the last year of the war, Sam was wounded."

Jack fidgeted in his chair.

Liko returned the medals to the old fisherman, who looked at them for a brief moment, then closed the blue box and placed it back in the drawer. He then picked up his tea cup and took a sip.

"Your great-grandson saw a ghost," Jack said.

The tea cup rattled in Yukio's old hands.

"He believes that rocks ward off ghosts," Jack continued. "Like garlic wards off vampires." He laughed. "I guess that's why he placed them around my porch. I imagine he put them around your house, too." Again Jack laughed, but it was an uneasy laugh. "He's afraid the ghost will take him away."

The old fisherman set down his tea cup, but not before tea sloshed onto the coffee table, just missing the base of his son's photo.

Seeing his sudden nervousness, Liko asked, "Have you seen the ghost, too?" With his napkin he wiped up the spill.

"Yes. The ghost is Ned's mother, Shelley. She returns to visit her son. She died giving birth, and now she returns."

Keahi and Jack looked at each other.

Liko noted that Shelley was a haole name. He wondered if Ned's mother was Caucasian, his father, Japanese.

"She wants to hold him. She has never held him in her arms. And now that Ned's father has joined her, she has returned for her son so her family can be together again."

Liko recalled that Ned's father had died in the head-on collision on the Big Island.

"I've seen this ... this woman," Jack said. His voice betrayed that his mind was visiting a sensitive memory. "She's not dead—not a ghost."

"Could she be the mother's sister?" Liko suggested. "A friend of the family? Someone who knows the kid?"

Yukio shook his head.

"Do you have a photo of the boy's mother?" Keahi asked.

"No."

"Look—I've seen this woman," Jack repeated. "She's haole and pale, which makes her look like a ghost. And it was late at night when I saw her. She has long, shiny black hair."

Liko saw the old fisherman's gnarled hands grip his chair and squeeze the wooden arms.

"Ned's mother died giving birth," Yukio repeated in a whisper.

"I'm sorry for your loss," Liko interjected.

"Thank you," Yukio said.

"My grandson raised Ned himself. One day he showed up with Ned, who was just learning to walk. My grandson said Ned had become too much responsibility. My grandson said he was between jobs, and he asked if I could take care of Ned, just for a while. I was reluctant. My wife had tended to these things, not me. But my grandson insisted."

He sighed a heavy sigh and shook his head, recalling unhappy events. "My grandson left without saying goodbye." Yukio jerked his head towards what must have been a bedroom, and then said, "He abandoned Ned."

He thought for a few moments, then added, "Ned is upset about the ghost. If I remove the rocks, it will upset him more."

He studied Jack. "I will make you a rock garden!" he said suddenly, a smile erupting on his weathered face. "Yes," his eyes sparkled. "You may keep the rocks, and I will make you a rock garden to keep away the ghost."

"What?" Jack said, a surprised expression on his face.

"I will make a rock garden in your front yard to protect you from the ghost!"

"But I told you, I don't believe in ghosts."

"But Ned does," Yukio said.

After further discussion Jack was talked into receiving a rock garden, but in his back yard, not in his front yard. It was also agreed that more rocks were needed, and since Yukio was getting along in years—he was even older than Jack!— he decided that Jack should collect the necessary rocks. So, at the urging of the old fisherman, Jack reluctantly agreed to hunt for suitable rocks. Of course Ned would help him!

Liko thought the outcome of the conversation was amusing. Jack and Ned would be tromping around together, an old man and a little boy, collecting rocks. He suppressed a chuckle. Ned and Jack reminded him of Dennis the Menace and Mr. Wilson in the TV series. It was all suddenly hilarious!

Yukio seems like an all right guy, too, Liko thought.

CHAPTER NINE

JACK SHOWED KEAHI HIS NEW OFFICE ornament: a 6-inch brown and black rock, lichen covered, in a shallow bowl near his desk. "It's a gift from my neighbor's great-grandson. Did Liko tell you about it?"

"He said something about ghosts and rocks and building rock gardens." Keahi smiled.

"I almost broke my neck. The little *menehune* put a rock right outside my front door."

Thinking that his smile may have been inappropriate, Keahi quickly redirected the conversation. "How's Liko working out?"

"Good, very good. He's a hard worker. He's put in long hours, and he never complains."

"I'm glad to hear that."

"Did you know that lichen is a unique life form—a combination of fungus and algae, both working together? The fungus stores water and the algae makes food?"

Keahi shook his head; he hadn't heard that. He'd gathered seaweed when he was a kid—he guessed that seaweed was algae—but he'd never thought about fungus, and certainly not lichen.

"Your nephew told me that," Jack continued. "He said it's a symbiotic relationship: they are helping each other, and both benefit."

Keahi watched Jack fill his mug with steaming coffee. *Why does everyone open up and trust this guy? It's definitely a gift,* he thought.

They sat down at a small, round table that was cluttered with paper. Jack sipped his hot coffee carefully. "I asked to see you this morning because I need your help." He blew across the top of the mug, dissipating the rising steam, rippling the surface.

Keahi shifted nervously in his chair. His tanned brow creased with concern. He had already spent several days filling out accident report forms and documenting how Kwon had been injured. He leaned back in his chair, feeling uneasy. He had no desire to revisit the accident yet again. He was at fault and he knew it. He just wanted HIOSH to conclude their investigation and for the Head of Department, Jack, to determine his punishment.

"Lim investigated the local labs and he uncovered a problem with one lab in particular."

"Really?" Keahi said, shifting his thoughts from HIOSH to the local labs. Lim had said nothing to him. In fact, Lim had reported nothing to the new team, either. "What did he find?"

"Well—" Jack tried to sip his coffee again, but it was still too hot, "—a mainland lab sent performance evaluation samples to all the labs that we use."

"Yes, that was the team's idea," Keahi said, nodding his head.

"Two labs failed," Jack said, continuing. "So Lim ran a second round of samples. The second time around he used our state lab. Our lab prepared samples of known quality and Lim delivered them to the two labs surreptitiously. The labs analyzed the samples and then reported the results to Lim."

Keahi could hardly believe what he was hearing. He bit his tongue, holding back his opinion of Lim.

"One lab failed."

"Which one?"

"Kalele Lab. It appears that Kalele Lab faked their results."

Damn! Keahi bit his tongue harder.

"I already called the Attorney General's Office. And I notified the Hawaii Bureau of Investigation."

Keahi's jaw dropped.

"Yes, the Bureau is now involved. We all met yesterday—the Attorney General, a criminal investigator from the Bureau, myself and Lim."

"And what happened?"

"Falsification of laboratory records is a felony," Jack said. "And using the mail to send falsified laboratory reports, that opens the door for the FBI."

"So it's now a federal case?"

"Yes."

Just like Kwon's case, Keahi thought. *We get creative, we investigate, and then the feds move in, take over, get all the credit.* "So, why are you telling me all this?"

"Because I need your help. Actually, I need your team's help." Jack tried his coffee again and found it cool enough to sip, just barely. "I need to know who used Kalele Lab and what decisions they made. I need the names of sites, property owners, consultants. I need a report by the end of the week. We need to know what the damage is."

Keahi raised an eyebrow.

"Yes. It appears that our department has been making decisions for years based on fraudulent data."

Stunned, Keahi tried to imagine the implications. "I'll get the information, but it will take some time."

Jack raised an eyebrow.

"We don't track that stuff—the names of consultants and what labs they used. We don't keep that information in a database."

"But it's in the files, hard copies, right?"

"Yes it is," Keahi said. "But we'll have to pull the reports, one at a time. It will be tedious."

Jack nodded.

Keahi ran into Lim in the bathroom. "You've been busy," Keahi said.

"No," Lim shook his head and shrugged his shoulders. "Not much happening."

"Really?" Keahi washed and dried his hands. "I heard you've been working hard."

"No, not really. What did you hear?"

Keahi stepped between Lim and the restroom door, though it was an unconscious move on his part. Nevertheless, he had cut off Lim's retreat.

It was an uncharacteristic move for Keahi and Lim stepped backwards, surprised. Keahi was a big guy and he was obviously upset. His arms were outstretched with his hands close to Lim's chest.

Lim took a step backward.

"I heard about the Bureau. And that the FBI has started a criminal investigation."

"Who told you that?" Lim's voice cracked.

"I heard that you used the state lab to finish the investigation. I heard that you met with the Bureau."

Lim's face paled.

"I heard that you took credit for everything." There was contempt in Keahi's voice.

"Hey, everything happened fast, I didn't have time to notify everyone, call a meeting. I had to keep the momentum going. Besides, I was just doing what you guys said to do—find out if there was a problem. And that's what I did."

"Did you give credit to the team?" Keahi asked, his voice conveying disappointment. He frowned and shook his head, pointing his index finger at Lim. With that, he turned and walked out the restroom door, leaving Lim standing in front of a row of dingy mirrors and dirty hand sinks.

The toilet flushed and Santos stepped out of a stall, startling Lim. "What's Keahi so mad about?"

"He's just overreacting. He's upset about a project I was working on."

"What project?"

Lim looked at Santos. "I guess it doesn't matter if I tell you. Now that Keahi knows, word will get out. Everyone will know by the end of the day."

"Know what?"

"A local lab is cooking data. I caught them, and the FBI is getting a search warrant."

"The federal—" Santos said, his throat constricting. "When will this happen?"

"Today. This afternoon. They are in federal court, right now, as we are talking, asking a judge for a search warrant."

"Which lab?"

"A local lab."

Santos turned away from Lim to look in the grimy mirror and saw sweat forming in small beads on his forehead. He turned on the cold water faucet and splashed lukewarm water onto his face. He was amazed at how fast his heart was fluttering. He ran both hands over his face, trying to hide his expression of total surprise.

"Everything has to be hush-hush until they execute the warrant. The police will probably search the lab tomorrow."

"Yeah," Santos said, drying his face with rough, recycled paper towels. "I understand." He was wheezing. "Everything has to be kept under wraps until the FBI executes the warrant." He coughed up some phlegm and spit it into the sink.

"You okay?" Lim asked.

"Just something I ate," Santos said.

Santos was furious. Someone should have told him about the lab investigations; if staff didn't keep their supervisors apprised of what they were doing, chaos would rule. But no one had said a word. Instead, he had learned about it in the restroom!

"They're messing with my reputation," he said out loud. His jaw tightened.

He waited until work ended and everyone had gone home, and then he crossed the hall to a door designated SUPPLY ROOM, which he found locked. He glanced nervously up and down the hall and clenched and unclenched his stubby hands. Pulling out his fat wallet, took out a key, unlocked the door and quickly stepped inside. He was breathing heavily. Closing the door, he switched on the light and negotiated his way past shelves filled with office supplies and boxes stacked haphazardly.

He quietly opened the far door and stuck his head into the Water Well Unit office, his body leaning forward to make up for the shortness of his fat, thick neck. The lights were off, so the light in the storage room, behind him, cast his heavy shadow. He let his eyes adjust to the darkness as he glanced around. It was quiet. Everyone had left.

He entered mumbling to himself: "Lim is to blame for this. And Keahi, too. If it takes a hundred years—"

He went to the front of the office and turned on the lights. By the time he got to Lim's cubicle he was puffing.

He ruffled through the papers on Lim's desk. Nothing. He looked through his four-drawer file cabinet. In the back of the top drawer he found a brown file labeled LAB PROJECT.

He sat in Lim's chair, opened the file, and read several pages. His lower back began to tighten and he blamed it on the old chair.

"Idiots," he said out loud, puffing and wheezing.

Even though he already knew why Alegado had insisted that he use Kalele Lab, it still disturbed him to see the concrete evidence in his hands.

His stubby hands trembled as he returned the file to Lim's file drawer. Then he hove himself out of the chair, turned off the office lights, passed back through the storage room, locked the storage room door, and returned to his own office. Puffing, he closed his office door and sat down at his desk.

The tightness spread from his lower back to the base of his neck as he mentally reviewed the facts. First, in years past, he had referred most of his sites to Kalele Lab. Second, the data from Kalele Lab was cooked. Third, Alegado, the Captain's consultant, had used the fraudulent data to write reports. Fourth, he—Santos—had used Alegado's reports to make decisions at several state-led cleanups. Consequently, buildings had been built upon contaminated properties. The child care center. A movie theater.

Could anyone fault Alegado for writing reports, drawing conclusions, making recommendations, all based on fraudulent data? Similarly, could anyone fault him for basing his decisions on Alegado's reports? He answered both questions in the negative—no one could blame Alegado or him—yet he felt no relief.

The important thing is to warn the Captain, he thought.

Sweat dripped from his brow onto his desk as he telephoned.

Alegado answered.

Santos mouth contorted as he said, "They know about Kalele Lab. Falsifying da kine."

"Say what, Santos?"

"Kalele lab! I'm talking about Kalele lab! They know the data's fake." *And that's just one felony.*

"Ahh . . ." Alegado said, his voice now reflecting that he understood.

A plume of gasoline underneath a playground.

He wheezed.

The fire.

He felt a shortness of breath.

The kids . . .

"Alegado, how many other bad sites are out there?"

"How long have we been working together, brah?"

Santos couldn't readily recall. *Has it been that long?*

"You take care of things on your end, Santos. I'll fix things on mine."

"Fix things," Santos said, incredulously. "How do you make contamination disappear?"

"The *oyabun* will fix it."

"The *oyabun?*"

Before Santos could say anything else, Alegado hung up.

Santos was stunned. "Idiot!" He slammed his phone into its cradle. His heart was racing. *Oyabun* was Japanese for godfather. The Captain was a shrewd business man, but he was no godfather.

Early the next morning, Santos said a few disparaging words to his wife, Mary, before she went to work next door in her residential care home. He kissed his daughter Lisa as she left for her teller job at the bank. Then he called into work sick.

He was now alone with his grandmother for the day, but she was not much company, for she had already fallen asleep in her La-Z-Boy in front of their big screen television. Her frail body almost disappeared in the large chair.

Listening to her softly snore, he raked his memory, recalling all the properties that he had referred to Kalele Lab. He picked up a notepad next to the telephone and scribbled down the names. The list quickly grew to eighteen.

In most cases it had been his influence as the supervisor that determined which lab was used; in almost every case Alegado had asked him to use Kalele Lab and he had agreed.

He ran the pencil down the list and underlined each site he thought could be a problem. He thought the words "new jail" looked funny framed by the notepaper's hibiscus border.

He underlined the Kesago Club twice. Two explosions had already occurred near the club: one in the playground, the second at the pet shop.

And there was the new movie theater, a multiplex. What would happen if there was an explosion and the theaters were packed? Would the roof fail? Would the high cinder block walls collapse?

Can I live with that? People crippled? People dead? What if it is someone I know? Do my daughter and her friends go there?

There was an upscale restaurant too, but Santos never wasted money on expensive dinners and fancy food. The last time he had taken his wife out to dinner was a long time ago—years ago.

I'll take her to dinner this weekend, he thought, suddenly feeling guilty. *She'll like that. However, I certainly won't take her to that restaurant.*

He folded the list and put it in his pants pocket.

Yesterday his lower back hurt. Today his chest muscles were tense. Sometimes he felt mopey, sometimes, depressed. He took two aspirins.

Later, mid-afternoon, his grandmother woke up and they had lunch together.

She was happy he had stayed home. In fact, she wanted to believe that he had stayed home to spend time with her, but she knew that wasn't true because he was drinking too much, as usual; by lunchtime, he had already finished a six-pack.

Nevertheless, she was proud of him. "Elpidio would have been proud of you, proud of the work that you do." Then, she talked about what a good man Elpidio was. "A man of principle," she said.

Santos listened passively, uninterested, his brain awash with beer. He said nothing about the list, but he was thinking hard about what to do with it. It was like a centipede at rest in his pocket.

Perhaps I should turn it in. That would make me look good. There is nothing illegal connecting me to the properties. So what if I reviewed Alegado's work? I have reviewed hundreds and hundreds of reports. I'm not responsible for the quality of the work done at the labs. That isn't my kuleana, my responsibility. And no one can trace this list back to me, provided I turn it in and act like I'm shocked. That I want all the properties investigated, cleaned up if necessary.

After lunch he retired to his big chair. He tried not to think about work and the Captain, but that only made it worse. *God I hate my job. I truly hate it.*

And he hated Jack, too. What authority did he have to investigate the labs? Yeah, he'd file a complaint about that, and he'd send copies of the complaint to his state representative and to the governor's office, too. *Yeah, this time I've got him.* But then he realized what a big mistake that would be.

Tired and full of food and beer, he closed his eyes and dozed off. When he woke up he asked his grandmother to bring him another beer. She did.

He failed to notice that her eyes were misty.

They watched Oprah.

When Picric Pete arrived just after midnight, Keahi was already at the scene watching the fire consume Kalele Lab. Multi-colored flames rose forty feet into the air.

"Surprised to see you here," Keahi said to Pete, "especially this late."

"I picked it up on my scanner."

"Miss the old job, huh?"

Pete shrugged.

They stared at the black smoke billowing from a large hole in the roof.

"A lot of chemicals in there," Keahi went on, raising his voice over the rumbling collapse of more roof.

"I haven't had a good night's sleep since I quit," Pete said.

They watched the fire.

The next day Santos decided to return to work. He was driving in, listening to the radio, when he heard that Kalele Lab had burned to the ground. He was so stunned he almost drove off the road.

The radio newscaster said firefighters were unable to save the lab. It was a total loss—the building, the equipment, and all the records. The newscaster said one firefighter had been injured, was treated at a local hospital, and released in fair condition.

When Santos arrived at work he pulled into his reserved space near the building and switched off the engine. He climbed out of his Buick and began walking towards the front door. His knees began to shake. For a moment he thought he would have to sit down in the parking lot on the asphalt.

His mind was reeling. *The Captain burned down the lab!* His legs were shaking. His world was spinning dangerously fast.

What a STUPID thing to do!

Later, Santos found himself seated at his desk but he was unsure how he had gotten there. He couldn't remember walking from the parking lot to his office.

Burning the lab down was tantamount to admitting fraudulent data. Yes, evidence had been destroyed. But now the feds would be much more interested!

The phone shrilled at him.

"Department of Water, Wind and Sun."

"How are you?" the Captain asked.

"Fine."

"Everything okay?" The Captain's voice sounded self-concerned and cold.

"Yes, everything is fine."

"Good. I am counting on you."

"Yes sir."

The Captain hung up.

Santos had trouble catching his breath. He was puffing hard. Dejected, he leaned back into his work chair.

"An oyabun fixed it," he mumbled.

CHAPTER TEN

ON MONDAY THE STAFF MET AT JACK'S beach house for a game of lawn bowling on his front lawn. The game was part of an agreement that Jack had negotiated with HIOSH: his department would pay a small fine and he would conduct training, with staff dressed-out in Level A protective suits. Most staff appreciated that Jack tried to make the training fun: that is, they would wear moon suits while lawn bowling. The staff also knew that the training was a consequence of Keahi and Kwon's ill-fated, improper entry into the pet shop without first donning proper personal protective equipment. Keahi had been placed on six months' probation.

Liko had been invited to help set up the bowling field, and he was happy to earn the extra cash; he needed the money for his dates with Toi. Besides, she was in the game, dressed in a splash suit, and he wouldn't miss that.

The players were now bowling in suits that were hot and uncomfortable. They all looked ridiculous, hilarious, Liko thought. And Keahi, whose suit was twice as large as everyone else's, looked especially silly. Keahi's full-body encapsulated suit was made of Tychem 9400—a very expensive, heavy, puncture- and tear-resistant material made by DuPont. He looked like a giant, shiny yellow parade balloon wearing small black gloves.

The old fisherman and his great-grandson Ned were rocking in solid teak chairs on Jack's front porch, trying to figure out the rules of the game. They sipped lemonade and laughed at the clumsy players. Ned was chewing dried strips of candied ginger. He loved the hot, spicy flavor and the pungent, citrus-like smell.

Yesterday morning, Sunday, the little kid had dropped in on Jack unannounced. He had opened Jack's front door, walked into his house, and awakened him in his bedroom.

Ned's surprise visits had started the day after their rock collecting venture. In fact, ever since that day, Ned had grown incorrigible. He appeared at Jack's house at all hours of the day, uninvited, unannounced, and always a surprise. And he never knocked; at daybreak one morning, Jack had nicknamed him *little rooster*—"My Little Chanticleer"—because he had pulled the sheets off Jack as he lay snoring in bed.

Consequently, Jack had invited the boy and his grandfather to the game, because he expected the little rooster would show up anyway, and he needed the old fisherman to keep Ned out of trouble. Jack did not want an unsupervised kid trampled by someone in a moon suit.

And now the two teams of four players were bowling the last end. As the lead bowler for his team, Keahi rolled a four-pound white target ball to the far end of the lawn, about fifty feet. The short roll wouldn't have qualified in a regulation game, but it was good enough for the day's effort.

Next, Keahi rolled two elliptical stone balls—genuine Hawaiian lawn bowling balls from his great-aunt's collection—as close as he could to the white target ball. One wobbled and went helter-skelter. Then Masako, the lead bowler of the opposing team, had her turn. She also had a pair of Keahi's antique elliptical balls.

After each player on both teams bowled two balls, the end was complete and everyone moon-suit-waddled to the far side of the field to argue the score. Masako's team won; they had more balls closer to the white target ball. They whooped and strutted boisterously with their inflated puffy arms raised towards the sky in proud victory, slapping each other's double-gloved hands in high-five congratulations.

After the last end, Liko collected his great-aunt's four antique bowling balls, took them up to the front porch, and set them under the picnic table away from everyone's feet. He felt a responsibility to protect them.

Then Keahi's team lined up and started through the mock decontamination exercise: outer gloves and boot covers were scrubbed with decontamination solution, duct tape around wrists and ankles was unwrapped, outer gloves were turned inside-out and taken off. After that, they scrubbed with a soft-bristled brush and rinsed off their yellow suits, inner green nitrile gloves, and heavy black boots. This mock decon continued until the splash suits were cleaned and packaged and ready for reuse. At the end of the line, they put on dry T-shirts and shorts and slippers.

In the meantime, waiting at the end of the slow-moving decontamination line, Keahi began to daydream.

He imagined that Masako, still wearing her splash suit, waddled over to the beach house and picked up the end of a garden hose. He fantasized that she turned the faucet on, crimped the hose back on itself so the water wouldn't spray, and carried it nonchalantly to the grassy field where her team was still hamming it up in their splash suits in post-game revelry, waiting their turn to enter the decon line. Lim was among them.

In his daydream, Keahi wondered, *Is she going to spray them?*

He watched as she waved to two other suits and they waved back.

"Lim," she ordered.

"Who, me?" A small splash suit stepped out from the end of the decon line and approached, his suit waddling side to side.

"Yes, you," Masako said. When Lim was within arm's distance she continued, "In special recognition—for being such a great team player—we give you the Green Cheese Award."

Suddenly two splash suits grabbed Lim's arms from behind. He yelled and he struggled but they wrestled him to the ground.

Masako sat on his chest. The trapped air in his suit ballooned his head and arms.

A third splash suit stepped forward holding a knife.

Lim yelled.

The knife cut a hole in the shoulder of Lim's suit. Air rushed out.

Masako stuck the end of the garden hose into the hole. "From all of us to you." She uncrimped the hose. Cold water sprayed into Lim's suit.

He yelled and tried to break away but the two suits held his arms and Masako scooted down onto his knees.

"You're not going anywhere," she said. She pinned his legs to the grass.

"Fill 'er up!" someone yelled.

"What are you doing to me?"

"Fluorescent yellow-green dye."

"You know, da kine for the sewers."

"Da kine turns rats green."

Someone laughed.

Masako held a large plastic bottle. She inverted it and stuck the nozzle into the hole in Lim's suit next to the garden hose. She squeezed, squirting and squirting a steady stream of bright yellow-green dye into the suit.

Lim struggled, wiggled.

And then a suit who was sitting on Lim's legs exclaimed, "Navy uses da kine as a marker at sea. One bottle marks an area the size of five football fields!"

"Turn off the water."

"We don't want to drown him."

"No worry. Da kine pop first."

Everyone laughed.

Lim was screaming bloody murder: "Let me out of here! Let me out of here! Help! Somebody help me! Please! Help me!"

"Stop struggling," Masako demanded.

She crimped the hose and pulled it out of his suit. Then all the splash suits jumped back, off of Lim, including Masako.

"Let this be a lesson," she said. "Next time think twice before you diss your team."

Someone pulled Lim to his feet. The water sloshed in his suit, settling in his boots and pants.

Keahi imagined Lim surrounded by his teammates in the middle of the grassy lawn, standing in a kid's wading pool stripped of his suit, standing in a puddle of green water. He imagined him naked except for his Speedo swim trunks, naked for all to see. And dyed yellow-green. A fitting punishment. Not only the Speedos but also Lim's birthday suit were bright fluorescent yellow-green. From head to toe—including his now green-freckled face –- he was green.

"My Speedos are ruined," Lim whined.

As soon as the fantasy ended, Keahi felt embarrassed and ashamed and unsatisfied. His hands were sweaty; his heart, racing; his breathing, fast and deep. He wanted to wipe his hands on his pants, but they were still encased in black gloves and he was still in the yellow moon suit.

But at least he could unclench his fists, and he did. And he could slow his breathing, and he did. He felt the pent-up anger slowly dissipate from his body. He even felt his chest muscles gradually relax.

Instead of getting the hose, as Keahi had fantasized, Masako bypassed the decontamination process, took off her suit, toweled hastily, and dressed. After pulling on plaid designer shorts and a T-shirt over her sweat-soaked swimsuit, she walked over to Liko, who was standing at the bottom of the porch steps. She remained barefoot. Touching Liko's shoulder she said, "I could use something cold to drink. Is there anything inside?" She tilted her head towards the front door of Jack's beach house.

"Soft drinks are in the kitchen," Liko answered, "in the refrigerator."

"Can you show me the way?"

Liko led her through the small cottage. An oscillating fan was stirring the dry, hot air. All the windows were open. In the kitchen they found Jack and Toi fixing sandwiches.

"Can we help?" Masako asked.

"No." Jack placed a slice of wheat bread on top of a sandwich, holding it in place gently with his hand and cutting it diagonally with a butcher knife. "This is the last one." He placed the sandwich with the others on the platter.

"Anything cold to drink?" she asked.

"How about lemonade?" Toi said. "I made a pitcher. Let me pour you a glass."

"If it's okay, I can get it."

"Cups in the cupboard," Jack said.

"And the lemonade's in the fridge," Toi added.

While Masako rummaged through the cupboard and found a package of red plastic cups, Liko took the pitcher of pink lemonade out of the refrigerator. She and Liko both drank a glass of fresh-squeezed lemonade as they watched Jack and Toi arrange the sandwiches on a large platter: mozzarella and beefsteak tomato on soft rolls; tuna salad on wheat; and turkey and avocado on sourdough.

They all went outside, each carrying something: Jack the sandwiches, Masako the red plastic cups and several bags of potato chips, Liko the pitcher of lemonade, and Toi a sack of melting, dripping ice. They set everything on a weathered redwood picnic table on the front porch.

By now, almost everyone had passed through the decon practice and had changed back into their street clothes. Hungry, they gathered and attacked the sandwiches.

Toi put ice in the red cups, poured the lemonade, and Liko began serving.

"Lemonade?" Liko asked Keahi. He was seated in a teak rocker next to the old fisherman and Ned.

"Thanks," Keahi answered. Liko walked over and handed his uncle a cup.

"God I'm thirsty." Keahi sipped the lemonade. "Those moon suits are terrible. I think I sweated two quarts." He had combed his hair and it was slicked back, wet.

Liko then served the old fisherman and Ned.

"Thanks," Ned said, setting down a half-chewed piece of ginger root. He grasped the large cup in his small hands, rocking slowly.

Meanwhile, Jack sat down next to Lim on the top porch step. Liko served them lemonade, too, and then started passing out the mozzarella with tomato sandwiches.

And then Santos arrived. No one had expected him to suit up; the consensus was that he would kill himself if he put on a moon suit and tried to breathe through a respirator. Even now he was huffing and puffing, having walked only from his car to the porch. Nevertheless, they had expected him to arrive on time. After all, he was a supervisor.

Santos sat down on his hippo-sized rump heavily, two steps below Lim and Jack. "Howsit?" he asked, turning to address everyone on the steps above him and on the porch.

Lim looked at Santos seated below him and gave a dull smile that conveyed the message, "Don't ask."

Then, before Santos could follow up on his question—which he would have done just to annoy everyone—Toi made an announcement, "Our team's in trouble. We spent all our money on the lab investigation." She paused and Liko noticed that she looked at Lim, who shifted his gaze from Santos to his slippers. "And now the department needs to investigate each property that used Kalele Lab."

"How do we do that?" Keahi asked.

"First we need to compile a list of all the properties that used Kalele Lab."

Santos put his hand in his pocket and caressed his list. He felt a sting of pleasure; the team was in trouble, and he had the power to help them . . . or not.

"And then we need to determine which properties are contaminated and unsafe."

Jack turned his body sideways on the steps so he could see Toi. She was standing above him, next to the picnic table on the porch, within arm's reach of the pitcher of lemonade and sacks of melting ice.

She concluded by saying, "If anyone has any ideas, knows how we can move forward, please let us know." And then she sat down next to Keahi in the fourth teak rocking chair.

Over lunch, the staff grumbled aimlessly about the arson. They talked and talked and talked but got nowhere. How unfortunate about the fire!

Bored, Liko was watching Toi. When she looked in his direction he quickly waved to get her attention. Then he spoke up, "Would anyone like to see Jack's new rock garden?"

"I would," Toi volunteered.

Need a chaperone? Keahi almost said. Instead, he watched, silently, as she joined Liko and they disappeared around the corner of the house, to the back yard. He wondered what his co-workers thought about his nephew's crush. Did they approve? Liko was only eighteen. But then he thought about Daniel, and then . . . he was almost happy for them.

Meanwhile Kwon drove up in his Kia and parked in the driveway along the side of the house. When he walked around to the front, his limp pained Keahi. More than six months had passed since the accident in the pet store, yet Kwon was still recovering.

Kwon stopped in front of the porch steps, standing in front of Santos and Jack and Lim. He was wearing a colorful Hawaiian shirt, tucked in, and yellow khaki shorts, held up by his signature rainbow suspenders. The Hawaiian shirt had a classic Buick motif, guaranteed to irritate Santos, Keahi thought, recalling Santos's oversized, over-air-conditioned Buick.

"Sorry for being so late," Kwon said, "but I wanted to finish compiling the list." He waved a brown folder over his head and he was smiling broadly, which Keahi knew was unusual.

"Excellent!" Jack said. Up until this point Jack had been unusually quiet, listening and observing. Now the sound of his voice—a reminder that the boss was among the workers—quieted the buzz of conversations.

"I found twenty-nine sites!" Kwon reported.

Santos reached into his pocket and crushed his list. He frowned; his opportunity had come and gone. He felt cheated.

"I checked the files, most of them, one-by-one." Kwon's voice radiated his excitement.

"We should computerize that stuff," Masako suggested.

Keahi watched Kwon's eyes follow Masako's voice up to where she was seated on the picnic table bench. His eyes betrayed his surprise at seeing her. It seemed to Keahi that Kwon's excitement suddenly deflated. His eyebrows came together and his mouth closed.

He began mumbling, his voice now self-conscious: "There were a lot of files ... and the air conditioning was cranked up ... it was freezing ... and the windows ... they're the kind that don't open." The folder was now hanging limply at his side, almost forgotten.

One moment he was excited, the next moment, nervous. Now dejected. What was the matter with him? *Why so mercurial?*

"I appreciate your hard work," Jack announced.

Keahi looked closely at Kwon. He was sweating profusely. He was also glancing around for a place to sit down. His scarred legs needed to rest. But the steps were taken and the rocking chairs were occupied. There was a seat on the bench next to Masako, but Keahi knew that would never happen!

"So what did you find?" Jack asked.

"You'd never guess." Kwon pulled the list from the brown folder and handed it to Jack. Bitterness crept into his self-conscious voice: "One of the sites is the Kesago Club— the former laundry site."

Keahi looked at Santos. Santos averted his eyes.

Jack read the list aloud. It included several restaurants, the new quarter-of-a-billion-dollar federal prison, and a multiplex theater.

"We need to investigate at least one of these sites," Kwon suggested.

"And how do we do that?" Masako asked.

Keahi noticed that Kwon flinched as if she was challenging him personally, which she wasn't. "I don't know," Kwon said. "We don't have any money."

Keahi saw several staff give Lim a disapproving glance.

"I spent what I thought was necessary," Lim said, defending himself. He raised his voice: "And I'd spend it again! Just the same!"

"Well," Kwon said, "If you had worked with us . . . ."

Lim started to reply but Santos spoke first. "Jack, what are you going to do about this mess?"

All side conversations stopped.

Jack was taken by surprise. "I don't have any special funds."

"So tell us, what are you going to do about it?" Santos asked again.

"That's up to the team now," Jack answered. "The team must decide."

"So you're cutting them loose?" There was rancor in Santos's voice.

"Well, I have an idea," Keahi volunteered.

"What?" Santos sneered.

"Kalele Lab won't be billing us for the samples they analyzed, right?"

Someone laughed, and then everyone else laughed, too.

"Actually, they'll probably bill us," Kwon said, "but that doesn't mean we'll pay, right? I mean, they are a bunch of crooks."

Keahi continued with a smile. "So that's the amount of cash we have left. Maybe, just maybe, we have enough for one more round of samples? So let's investigate one of the sites on Kwon's list. You guys choose the site. I know which one I'd choose!"

"The Kesago Club!" everyone said in unison.

"Yes!" Keahi burst out. "If Jack agrees we'll investigate the Kesago Club. I'll set it up."

"Well," Jack said, "Santos, you are the supervisor of the remediation unit. What do you say?"

"Um," he hesitated.

Everyone was quiet while Santos considered Jack's question.

"That's fine with me," he said, finally. "It's my program though, so I will take the lead. And I will use my own staff." Thus he dismissed the team without even acknowledging them. "And Keahi, since you are on probation, I don't want you involved. Period. You can continue with your current assignment: organize and digitize the files. Like Masako said, we need to computerize."

The public rebuke was so painful that Keahi almost resigned, but he let himself go numb instead.

"I'll expect regular updates," Jack told Santos. "The first week of each month."

At that moment, Liko and Toi returned from their walk. They stopped next to Kwon, in front of the team. "Have you guys seen the rock garden?" Toi asked, interrupting. She looked past Santos and Lim and Jack, and addressed the old fisherman in the teak rocking chair: "It's nice. You did a wonderful job."

Yukio nodded acknowledgement, then said, "Jack and Ned collected the rocks—together." He reached out and patted his great-grandson on the head. "I only arranged them."

When Toi described the garden, her enthusiasm convinced everyone that they had to see the rocks too, so they all walked around the house to the back yard and were soon admiring the rock garden and complimenting Jack and the old fisherman and the boy.

"Wouldn't a rock garden look great in our courtyard?" Toi asked Jack, earnestly.

She turned to the old fisherman. "Yukio, we have a courtyard at work. We have a recycled picnic table. A few young fruit trees. But no rocks."

"I would be pleased to create a garden for you," the old fisherman volunteered, willingly.

All eyes turned to Jack. He said, "Yukio, that is a most generous offer. But as you just heard, we are broke. How could we pay you?"

"I don't need money," the old fisherman said. "All my needs are taken care of. I have a roof over my head and fish from the sea."

"But we would not expect you to build a garden without compensation."

"Compensation?" The old fisherman stroked his chin several times, then, with a mischievous smile said, "No compensation, but one request."

He's up to something, Liko thought. *He's a smart guy.*

"What is your request?" Jack asked.

"You must collect the rocks with my great-grandson."

"Oh, I see," Jack said, a grin spreading across his face. "More rocks. That's the hardest part, you know—running around looking for rocks. And once I find them, I have to move them, carry them around. Yeah. And some are heavy."

Seeing Jack so easily finessed, everyone laughed.

"And each of you must contribute one nice rock, too," the old fisherman said, rhythmically pointing his finger at each person admiring the garden, as if counting them.

Everyone agreed to participate, except Santos. After all, he had filed a grievance regarding the use of the public courtyard for a meeting area. Jack announced that a rock garden was landscaping. And keeping the courtyard landscaped was not a change of use.

By next Friday, each person would leave one large, special rock in the office courtyard. Together, Jack and Ned would collect any additional rocks that were needed. And then the old fisherman would build another rock garden.

"Idiots," Santos mumbled, but not loud enough to draw attention. "We have a crisis and you're talking about rocks?"

Liko, for his part, decided that he would create a vegetable garden on the side of Jack's house while Yukio built the rock garden. He would model it after the community gardens that he had seen near his uncle's place. Besides, he had discovered that he enjoyed working outdoors with his hands.

CHAPTER ELEVEN

Liko carefully leaned the garden rake against the inside wall of the wooden shed, next to the shovel and hoe. Then he studied his hands. They were covered with dry red clay and when he closed and opened them the caked clay on his palms and fingers cracked. It was a new experience and he liked it.

For some weeks, he had been making his vegetable garden at the side of Jack's beach house—the side opposite the old fisherman's cottage, the side that received full sun and was shielded from the dry winds by a wild *haole koa* windbreak. It was a large, ambitious garden with eight raised growing beds, each four feet wide by ten feet long by one foot deep.

He had spent two weeks preparing the heavy soil. First he had broken the surface of the dry ground with a spade, turning under a rank growth of tall, scraggly weeds. After that he built the wooden frames for the raised beds, three feet apart, in two parallel rows containing four beds each. Jack had trucked in black topsoil from agricultural land that was being covered with cement slabs and house foundations. And then Liko had shoveled the rescued topsoil into the raised beds.

Today he had mowed Jack's front yard, collecting the dry grass clippings and tossing them into a chicken wire compost bin, which he had built with lumber left over from the raised beds. After that, dismayed by the worn condition of the garden tools, he had sharpened the shovel and hoe and rake. He was learning how to care for tools.

He stepped out of the shed and saw the sun was an orange ball sitting on the horizon. The soft sunlight set the wooden sides of the raised beds aglow.

He walked over to the garden hose at the back of Jack's house and took off his T-shirt, which he hung on the head of a rusty nail above the faucet. He washed his hands and splashed his face. He held the hose overhead and let the cool water pour over the back of his head and neck. It felt wonderful and refreshing.

When he looked up, he saw a pale woman with long black hair, barely dressed, watching him from the other side of the hibiscus hedge in the old fisherman's yard. It was unmistakable: she was watching him. And she was practically naked.

Without taking his eyes off her, he shook the water from his hair like a dog. He turned his head to grab his shirt off the rusty nail—only a few seconds—and when he looked back, she had disappeared.

He ran to the hibiscus hedge, searched until he found Ned's passageway, and squeezed his large body through, scratching his arms and neck. Once through, his eyes swept the yard where he had last seen her, behind the old fisherman's cottage, near the tangle of hau tree branches. She had to be there, hidden in its convoluted branches. He went directly to the tree and raced around it. She had vanished.

"Hello," a startled voice called. He spun sideways and faced the old fisherman standing in the back door of his cottage.

"Did you see her?" Liko pulled his T-shirt on.

"Who?" he asked in a friendly voice. "I didn't see anyone."

"I saw her!" Liko said. "She was here, then she was gone."

"Ned!" Yukio exclaimed. An expression of worry clouded his face. "I must check Ned!" He turned and hurried back into the cottage with Liko close behind.

They found Ned playing Legos under his bed.

Once they were sure that Ned was okay, they quickly searched each room in the small cottage, but found nothing. So they went outside again and Liko rechecked the hau tree, thoroughly, and then they looked behind every bush and every tree within a hundred feet of the cottage. But the pale woman had vanished.

"A ghost," Yukio mumbled.

"No such thing," Liko countered. "I saw her. She's real."

They went back inside the cottage and Liko phoned Jack. He immediately came over.

At first Jack appeared upset, but then he seemed relieved. "Maybe it's best we don't catch her. What does one say to a ghost?"

Liko looked at him inquiringly.

"Especially a ghost who appears just before the sun sets," Jack added. He smiled sadly.

Liko noted that it was, indeed, turning dark.

They talked about her in the small kitchen while the old fisherman fixed a pot of tea. Then they collected the teapot and cups, and little Ned and a large box of Legos, and moved to a table under the splendid old hau tree in the back yard. Yukio made another quick trip inside, returning with a battery-powered Coleman lantern attached to a short rope. He tied the bright light to a hau branch.

They settled around the table and Ned slipped underneath, corralled by their feet, to play in the shadows with his Legos.

The old fisherman poured tea. "Did you know that your father and I were friends?" he asked Jack.

A quizzical expression crossed Jack's face.

"In our youth, your father and I were both issei from the same small village in Japan."

"My stepfather, you mean?"

Yukio examined Jack closely for a moment. "In his youth, your stepfather was ambitious. I wanted to be a fisherman, just like my father before me and his father before him." He adjusted himself in his seat. "But your stepfather, he wanted his own business. He believed that if he started his own business, if he worked hard, then he would become wealthy and respected."

"Sounds like the American Dream," Jack said, his voice betraying his sarcasm.

"Yes, your stepfather—my friend—was a dreamer."

There was a clattering of Lego pieces. Liko glanced under the table. He saw Ned throw the Lego box aside and spread the Legos in the sand and decaying hau leaves.

Liko wondered if there might be centipedes or other crawling creatures in the leaves. Should he bring it to Yukio's attention?

"He started his own business." Yukio said. "And he worked hard."

"Started his own business?" Jack said in a snide tone. "You mean my mother set him up in business with her own money."

"Yes, that is true."

Jack looked at Liko. "And he lost everything."

Yukio was quiet for some seconds, and then he responded. "If you are angry at your stepfather then you should be angry at *me*, not at him."

"Why is that?"

"Because I persuaded him to accept her money."

Jack's jaw dropped, literally, and he stared at Yukio.

"Your stepfather came to me and asked my advice. Your mother had sold her family farm and offered him the money—to bankroll him.

"You see, it was her idea, not his, to use the money for the new business. He would never have asked her. After she offered him the money he came to me and asked my advice.

"All his life he had wanted his own business, but in those days it was difficult to save investment capital. He had saved some money, but not enough. He did not feel right taking her money, even though they were married. Besides, he knew it was your inheritance, Jack. So he told your mother to invest the money. But your mother insisted he start a business. That is when your stepfather sought my advice."

"Why would he seek *your* advice?" Jack asked.

"Because we were friends. And because," Yukio smiled proudly, "at that time I had a successful business—I had a fishing boat."

"So what happened?" Jack asked.

"I told him 'Don't start a trust fund.'"

"Damn!" Jack shook his head, his eyes locked on the old fisherman.

"I knew your stepfather. Like I said, I knew him from our youth."

"Yes, yes, you said that already."

"And I knew his dream. He had studied other people's businesses, and he understood why they had succeeded or failed. He was a hard worker. He was smart. I was confident his business would be successful—that it would make him, and you, and your mother, wealthy and respected."

Little Ned crawled out from under the table and into Jack's lap, surprising him. "What do you want, little rooster?" Jack groaned under the weight of the boy. Ned enthusiastically handed him a Lego creation. Jack turned it over in his hands, trying to figure out what in the world it was supposed to be, and then gave it back. "Very inter-esting," he said.

"It's a rock!" Ned shouted with pride.

Jack smiled painfully. "I see."

Ned leaned back against Jack's chest and snuggled into the warmth of his old frame. Liko imagined arthritic bones popping like cracked knuckles. And the smell of apples and smoky peat.

"So I am to blame that you lost your inheritance," Yukio said to Jack. "Not your stepfather."

"Well, the timing could not have been worse," Jack said.

"What was wrong with the timing?" Liko asked, joining the conversation.

"He opened the business in the summer of '41," Jack answered.

Liko looked puzzled, so the old fisherman explained: "The Japanese bombed Pearl Harbor in December."

"Oh," Liko said, nodding his head.

"They were both proud of the new business," Yukio added.

"I can forgive him taking her money," Jack said, his voice gone flat. "I can understand that. But I can't forgive him for investing in Japanese War Bonds."

Little Ned was now pulling the Legos off his "rock" and thumping them down on the table like mahjong tiles.

"And several months later," the old fisherman said, once again explaining to Liko, "Japan attacked Pearl Harbor."

"Yes," Jack said, raising his voice, slightly. "And he lost everything: the new business, the investment in the Japanese War Bonds, everything."

"What happened to the war bonds?" Liko asked.

"The U.S. froze his bank account," the old fisherman answered for Jack. "The federal government closed down the American branches of Japanese banks."

"But why did he lose his business?" Liko asked, still puzzled.

"Bad timing," the old fisherman explained. "Downtown Honolulu was unfavorable to a new Japanese business right after Pearl Harbor was bombed."

"I see," Liko said.

"When he returned home from the internment camp, he was a broken man," Yukio added. "His business had failed. His investments were worthless. He was in debt. His entire world was destroyed."

"I didn't know that he had been sent to a detainment camp," Jack said. "I learned about it only a few years ago, through some relatives."

Liko thought the old fisherman studied Jack for a moment. "I saw him shortly after his return. He asked about you, whether I had news about you. He said your mother had not seen or heard from you since you joined the Marines. He said you had not returned home after the war, and your mother did not know where you were living."

"I didn't keep in touch," Jack said.

"He did not live long after that." Yukio was now explaining the events to Liko. "They moved into a small apartment in downtown Honolulu. Shortly afterwards, he had a stroke. Mercifully, he died three months later."

"Did the family attend the funeral?" Jack asked.

The old fisherman hung his head low. "No, no one came."

"I've always wondered," Jack said. He explained to Liko, "When she married my stepfather, her family ostracized her."

"And when the business failed," the old fisherman added, "they blamed it all on your stepfather, although she defended him steadfastly, which caused an even deeper rift."

"How do you know that?" Jack asked.

"She told me. After he died, she moved from town to the beach house." Yukio nodded towards Jack's beach house. "I was already living here in this cottage. It was an arrangement I had with your stepfather. The house was to be their vacation home: a place to retreat. I was to live in the cottage and take care of the house."

"Well, at least he made one good investment," Jack said.

"This was a good place for a Japanese fisherman like me; it was isolated from the soldiers, yet close to Waianae Boat Harbor, where I kept my boat."

"So when my mother moved out here, she allowed you to stay?"

"Yes, she *asked* me to stay," the old fisherman recalled. "I don't know why. Perhaps I was the last connection she had with her husband."

Yukio added, "One day she told me, 'When I sold the farm, he insisted I buy this cottage for myself, as our vacation home. I thought it was so silly, but he insisted. And now this is all I have left.'"

Jack nodded. He remembered that his mother had called this beach house their vacation home.

"Why did he invest in Japanese War Bonds?" Liko asked.

"Because he was proud of his Japanese roots, his homeland, everything Japanese."

"He was proud of Japan's conquests in China," Jack corrected, in a derogatory tone. "He read the *Nippu Jiji* daily, a Japanese Hawaiian newspaper. I can hear him now, as if he were right here with us, going on and on about Japan's victories in China. It filled him with pride."

"So investing in Japanese War Bonds was his way of supporting Japan's war in China?" Liko asked.

"Yes," Jack said. "What he didn't spend on the business, or on this vacation home, he spent on Japanese Imperial War Bonds."

"And he lost everything when Pearl Harbor was attacked?" Liko asked.

"Yes," the old fisherman said, "but no one knew that Pearl Harbor would be attacked. I myself disagreed with your father about the war bonds. We had an argument. I told him he should not support Japan's military. He should not support Japanese imperialism. But he said it was inevitable Japan should conquer not only Korea, but also China. He believed that it was Japan's duty to civilize the Koreans and the Chinese." Yukio cleared his throat self-consciously. "Yes, I remember that that is the word he used, 'civilize.' Japan's mission was to civilize its neighbors. I did not invest in Japan's bonds. But the investment was not reckless."

"Not reckless?" Jack objected. "He lost everything!"

"Yes," the old fisherman said. "And the FBI arrested him."

"Because of the war bonds?" Liko asked.

"Yes," the old fisherman answered. "He was very proud of Japan."

"So your stepfather supported Japan instead of the United States?" Liko asked Jack.

Jack shrugged.

"We will never know the answer to that question," the old fisherman said in a flat tone.

"Why is that?"

"Because he was denied the freedom to make a choice, to choose his allegiance: to serve either Japan or to serve the United States."

"Everyone had a choice, didn't they?" Liko asked.

"The FBI arrested him before he made a declaration one way or the other," the old fisherman said. "And after he was arrested and taken away to the detention camp, he never made the choice."

"I don't know about that," Jack said. "It was rather clear to me. The last time I saw him, that day, I argued with him about joining the Marines and he said no."

Jack turned to Liko and explained. "It was less than a week after the Japanese attacked Pearl Harbor. I approached my stepfather and asked his permission to join the Marines. I was only seventeen years old, so I needed his permission.

"He refused. He would not even discuss it."

"He gave you no reason?" Liko asked.

"He said, 'No, I will not allow you to fight against the great nation of Japan and our family, our relatives, and our friends.' I remember my mother entering the room in the middle of our argument. She did not want me to leave home either, so she sided with my stepfather. We exchanged some heated words, and then I ran away. I never saw them again."

Jack recalled how pale his mother looked when he told her that he wanted to enlist. She had long black hair. It was just before breakfast when he made his declaration and she was still in her night clothes. She looked so pale, so fragile, so ghostly.

"I remember how hurt I was. I recall telling her: 'I don't love you. I don't even like you.' For that, I have never forgiven myself."

Jack sighed and said, "You know, when I saw Ned's mom—or her ghost—it reminded me of my mother, fifty years ago!"

There was an awkward silence that lasted for quite a while.

"Your stepfather and I were very good friends," Yukio said. "When my son, Sam, and I returned to shore—we were out fishing and saw the first Japanese planes fly over—we docked and immediately drove home. Your father greeted us. He had driven all the way out here, as if he were trying to flee from what had happened. He was overwrought, near hysterics. He said it was a great tragedy. He said it would be the end of

Japan. There was no question in his mind that Japan would be defeated. He was upset because he knew it would be a terrible loss for both sides, but especially for Japan."

"He had a Samurai sword with him—a sword that had been handed down in his family for many generations. I saw him destroy the sword in shame and dismay, right here at the beach house."

"I guess it was several days later I asked his permission to join," Jack said. "I asked him to sign the waiver. I told him I wanted to fight the 'dirty Japs.' I was angry and bitter and full of hatred. I guess he knew that Japan would be defeated without my help."

"I have one more thing I must tell you," the old fisherman said. "Something your mother told me. That day, after you left, your stepfather collected all of his Japanese belongings and burned them. That is what your mother told me. He burned them in their backyard. Then your father told her he would find you and bring you back home."

"He must not have looked very hard," Jack said. "After all, I only ran as far as Honolulu to join the Marines. I was under-age and he knew where I was going, what I was doing. It would have been very easy to find me, to have my enlistment nullified."

"But that day," the old fisherman said, "that is the same day that the FBI came and arrested him.

"Your mother didn't see him for a long time," the old fisherman added. "Later she told me that she had lost both of you on that day."

Jack sat under the hau tree in silence. He had nothing more to say. That day there had been a terrible rift between him and his parents and he had never seen either of them again, despite the many years that had passed. It was foolishness and a great folly on his part.

They remained quiet for some time, except for little Ned who was still playing with his Legos.

Liko left Jack's beach house around ten o'clock and drove across the island to Keahi's studio on Pualei Circle in an old white Camry that his great-aunt had loaned him. He had planned on getting back earlier, but he had not expected the conversation between the old fisherman and Jack to last so long, or to be so interesting. They were still sitting under the hau tree when he left, still talking story, still wondering who the strange woman—or ghost—was. Eventually, little Ned had fallen asleep among his Legos and the old fisherman had tucked him into bed, returning to the table under the hau tree with a bottle of saki. Liko had taken that as his cue to leave. He had wanted to stay—they might have shared the saki with him—however, he had promised Keahi that he would be home at a reasonable hour. And now it was almost midnight!

As he drove through Waikiki, he thought about Jack's relationship with his mother and stepfather. What a tragic story. It seemed so uncharacteristic of Jack. How could he possess such understanding, such empathy, such emotional intelligence, yet be so cold and so unforgiving towards his own mother and stepfather? Liko found it unfathomable.

It was after midnight when he finally pulled into the covered parking area on the ground level, beneath the building's spacious, two-bedroom condominiums. The engine roared, the brakes squealed, the steering whined. He parked the Camry in one of two stalls under the manager's condominium and cut the engine as quickly as possible.

When he jumped out of the car, he absentmindedly slammed the door. He grimaced as the metal-on-metal "wham" bounced off the concrete walls and echoed. He expected a dog to bark but there was only silence.

He stepped to the white fence, reached over the top of the wooden gate, unlatched a simple hook, and swung the gate open to the courtyard and pool. He quietly walked across the flagstone decking towards Keahi's building, the one that contained the studio rentals, passing in front of the sliding glass doors of the one-bedroom condominiums in the adjoining building. Reaching a plumeria tree and the outdoor stairway, he climbed to the third floor walkway. The sky was cloudy, with no moon or stars visible.

When Liko reached the front door of his uncle's studio, he picked up the *Star-Bulletin* off the bare concrete walkway. It was unusual for the evening paper to be left outside, unread, but Keahi had not been feeling well, and Liko recalled that earlier in the morning Keahi had been shuffling around the kitchen, sniffling and complaining about a headache. *Maybe he's come down with a cold*, Liko speculated. *Or worse, the flu.*

Standing outside the studio, Liko slipped off the red rubber band and opened the paper in the dim yellow glow of an incandescent bulb. He skimmed the headlines.

YOUTH DROWNS IN LAVA TUBES! screamed from the front page.

Stunned, he stood under the naked bulb, reread the headline, skimmed the text, found what he didn't want to find.

He opened the front door with his guest key and entered the small studio. He heard Keahi in bed, snoring. If he was sick, he was now getting some rest, so Liko did not disturb him.

He went into the bathroom, softly closed the door, and flicked on the light. He sat on the closed toilet and read about the drowning.

The young man at the dive shop, who filled his tanks with air, who had asked him to be his buddy, had drowned. There had been three divers. "I'm the missing buddy," he said to himself. "I should have been there."

When he finished, he folded the paper in half and set it on the back of the toilet tank. He splashed water on his face and mindlessly brushed his teeth. He stripped down to his underwear, peed, washed his hands.

He returned to the studio room, carried the coffee table across the room to the far wall, and opened the large hide-a-way bed, as quietly as possible.

He felt numb. He dropped his tired body onto the bed and lay awake, listening to Keahi snore. A few hours later he finally fell asleep, but only long enough to dream—to relive his own disastrous quarry dive.

In his nightmare, he smiled at the pretty girl as they passed on the surface of the quarry. She smiled back, though nervous. He had finished his dive; she was beginning hers.

In the nightmare Liko had something he needed to tell her. Something she needed to know. But he couldn't find the words.

When he reached the wooden platform, he climbed out of the water onto the rotten wood deck. He looked back towards the buoy at the center of the quarry, but the dive instructor and the girl were already gone. Upset with himself, he systematically removed his dive gear, setting it piecemeal on the gray weathered planks of the dock.

Later he heard panic in the voices of the other students. They had been watching the dive while he was removing his gear.

"What's the matter?" Liko asked.

"She hasn't come up!" someone whispered.

"And the dive instructor?"

"He can't find her."

The dive instructor surfaced, yelling to the students, "Get help! Quick! Get help!"

Liko heard panic and fear in the dive instructor's voice. Help? From where? It would take minutes to get to a phone. Liko stood on the dock, frozen.

Later they found the girl's body, her dive gear caught on an old motorcycle's handle bar, sixty feet below the surface.

Liko awoke from the nightmare and checked his watch: 4:35am. For a long time he lay in bed, listening to the familiar sound of Keahi snoring and the whirl of the ceiling fan.

He got up and quietly left the studio.

He walked across Kapiolani Park, passed under the row of old ironwood trees planted more than a hundred years ago, and took a seat on a bench overlooking San Souci Beach. It was the same bench where he had met Toi the summer before, but now, at this early hour, it was deserted.

Fairy terns, bright white, were riding the air currents, rising from the ocean, soaring high into the clear sky. The first light of the rising sun reflected off the terns as they swooped and danced and climbed, higher and higher. He listened to their chatter. Their high pitch reminded him of Toi.

He glanced over at the beachside showers but no one was there. Of course he knew Toi wouldn't be there, but . . . .

He recalled how the water had sparkled around her like silver confetti catching sunlight. He watched the fairy terns fly out of sight.

Keahi had been at work only a few minutes, when Toi popped unexpectedly into his cubicle. She had an office copy of the *Honolulu Advertiser.*

"Have you seen this?" she asked.

"Seen what?" Keahi blew his nose. He had a summer cold and hated it.

Toi handed him the *Advertiser.* YOUTH DROWNS IN LAVA TUBES.

"My God!"

"Does Liko know?"

"He was gone when I got up."

"Gone? Where?"

"I don't know." Keahi was getting testy about the interrogatory tone of Toi's questioning. "Swimming?"

"First thing in the morning?"

"Maybe."

"I think you had better call him."

He was unprepared for the barrage of concern and worry that Toi was dumping on him. Keahi thought for a moment. He started to say, "He's old enough to...," but stopped mid-sentence.

He called Liko at the studio. There was no answer.

Prompted by Toi, he took emergency sick leave and went directly home.

He found that Liko had put up the hide-a-bed and had returned the coffee table to its usual place. Keahi looked in the closet. Liko's clothes were no longer on the hangers. He stepped into the bathroom and discovered Liko's toiletries were gone.

He saw a folded newspaper on the back of the toilet tank. He picked it up and re-read the headline, YOUTH DROWNS IN LAVA TUBES.

He looked under the bed for Liko's new suitcase. It was missing.

He went to the refrigerator and grabbed two large cans of Foster's Lager and stepped out onto his lanai. Then he sat down in the loveseat, popped open a can and guzzled it. He set the empty can on the glass top of his lanai table.

He felt miserable.

After drinking the second Foster's, he called Toi.

"I told you," she said, angrily.

"He's probably flown home," Keahi said, trying to calm her.

After a short conversation, he hung up and returned to the lanai with two more Foster's. He said out loud, as if talking to himself, "You do what you think is right, and the ones you love get hurt anyway."

He drank another beer.

He blew his nose for the hundredth time that day, but this time it wasn't because of his cold.

CHAPTER TWELVE

GREAT-AUNTIE SHOWED LIKO A PICTURE of herself in a cyber-green snow outfit, racing down the slope, trying out her new skis in powdery snow. "This year's trip to Steamboat."

They were seated beside each other on a large couch in her back yard. In front of them was the Pacific. To their right and left were walls of bougainvillea, bright magenta, bright orange, thorny, greater than ten feet tall, climbing the black lava-rock walls that separated her beachfront property from her neighbors. Behind Liko and his great-aunt was her home and her priceless collection of Hawaiian antiques.

Liko studied the picture. She was not wearing a helmet. *Reckless of her,* he thought. He noticed the changes in her appearance since her youth. Gone were the coiled black braids, replaced now by her natural grey hair cut short in a Peter Pan style. With her youthful personality and her five foot two-and-a-half inch height, she easily could have passed for Peter Pan—a Hawaiian version of Peter Pan. But on snow skis!

"Join me next winter?" she suggested. "I'll sign you up for classes."

After spending most of his life in a trailer park just outside Las Vegas, and the last two summers in Hawaii, Liko couldn't imagine skiing in the mountains. "Thanks, but my passion is the ocean, scuba diving."

"And thanks again for the buoyancy control jacket." He reached out and lightly touched her tanned forearm. She had given him the jacket last summer, during his first summer visit. At that time he couldn't swim, so he had greatly appreciated the jacket. It had enabled him to float when it was inflated.

She returned his smile and nodded, which was her way of saying "You're welcome." Her eyes sparkled.

"You still have a personal fitness trainer?" he asked.

"Three times a week."

"And a yoga teacher?"

"Wednesday and Fridays."

"And Pilates?"

"The Pilates instructor, she and her daughter are always late, sometimes they don't even make it."

"And half an hour on the treadmill followed by a swim in the ocean."

"Every day."

"Well, well. You should live to 110." They laughed together, sharing the family chuckle.

"I'm serious," she said. "You can move into Keahi's old room, finish your senior year here."

He frowned. He had already told Great-Auntie about the drowned boy, so she knew that he had asked Liko to be his dive buddy. She also knew that Liko was upset because Keahi had refused to let him dive the lava tubes and because Toi had sided with Keahi.

"Thank you, but I have decided to return to Mom's." He couldn't restrain the sigh. The trailer park outside Las Vegas was not a place that he wanted to return to; in fact, it was the place that he had been trying to escape as long as he could remember.

He said, "I learned a lesson from Jack, Keahi's boss." He told her that when the Japanese had bombed Pearl Harbor, Jack was his age, seventeen. She raised an eyebrow when he said that. And she tracked the story when he told her about Jack's falling-out with his mother and stepfather.

He continued, "It's sad, but Jack never returned home and he never saw his parents again. Now they are both dead. As a result, he's been carrying terrible baggage around with him, ever since he was my age, and now for his whole life. I don't want that."

Liko smiled sadly. "When I left Mom's, I never planned on returning. But now, well, I know that's a trap. I'd carry a lot of baggage around with me the rest of my life, too. And I don't want that."

"But you are not responsible for your mother," his great-aunt said. "You understand that, don't you?"

"I'm worried about her. I can't leave her in that trailer, in that trailer park." He looked at his great-aunt. "I need to find her a better place to live. Set her up in an apartment, or something."

Great-Auntie's countenance suddenly glowed as if lit up from within. "I'm proud of you, Liko!" Her eyes moistened. "Let me make you an offer."

"Okay," Liko said, diffidently, raising an eyebrow. "What?"

"Do you still want to travel, see the world?" She chuckled. "That was your goal last summer."

Great-Auntie's laugh filled him with warmth. "Oh yes! But I have also discovered the ocean." He gazed out to the ocean and followed a windsurfer skipping along the surface. "I feel this relationship . . . . But yes, I still want to travel."

"Then consider this." She locked Liko's eyes to hers. "Convince your mother to sell her trailer. Move her into an apartment. And then, after you graduate from high school, give me a call."

He nodded agreement.

"If you still want to travel — to discover the world — then I will provide you the resources."

"Wow! That's fantastic!"

"Of course," she said, "after your travels, you may decide to pursue oceanography or marine biology or perhaps something else at the university." She smiled and again chuckled. "Time will change you, Liko. But don't concern yourself with that right now. I will help you attend whatever school you choose."

"Thank you," he said.

She placed her small hand on top of his and patted several times, softly.

"How is Keahi?" she asked.

"He's not very happy."

Her lips pursed and she exhaled with sadness. "No, I expect not. Something needs to happen to wake him up. I was hopeful that your visit would help. But it wasn't enough."

"What do you mean?"

"Seeing you in all your youth. I hoped it would remind him of all that he has set aside. You see, he also had dreams. He loved to sing and dance and perform. But instead, he has chosen to sit in an office—a cubicle. His personality is not that of a government employee. If only he would awaken!"

"Yes, I can see that." *And he's drinking, heavily.*

"How is your girlfriend?"

"Toi? Fantastic. She taught me buoyancy control." Liko smiled, sheepishly, realizing that he had just revealed to his great-aunt that he had not learned the basic buoyancy control skill until this summer.

"She loves the ocean, too. Keahi nicknamed her 'Little Ama' which has something to do with divers."

"Little Ama and Little Nene," Great-Auntie said.

Liko blushed, suddenly remembering the story of how his great-aunt had called him Little Nene during one of her visits to their trailer, when he was so protective of his mother. Since then, he had seen the pugnacious Hawaiian geese defending their nests in the Honolulu Zoo.

"I'm going to call her later tonight and see if she can join me tomorrow, for lunch."

"When do you leave?"

"Tomorrow night. I always seem to get the red-eye flights."

"And Keahi?"

Liko hadn't decided whether or not to call Keahi before he left. Tonight he would spend at his great-aunt's and tomorrow he would see Toi for lunch, hopefully. "Keahi? I don't know."

When the lights went out in the house and he thought that his great-aunt had gone to bed, he left his bedroom and wandered through her living room, which could just as likely be called a museum. He found the warrior mask and warrior club, and especially the warrior bowl on the glass shelves protected in a locked china cabinet-like display case. A small shiny key had been left in the lock and it clicked as he turned it. The glass door opened easily.

First he picked up the warrior club. He ran his finger along the sharp edges of the shark teeth inlaid along its perimeter. He admired the weight of the club, moving it up and down in the air.

He set the club down and with both hands picked up the warrior bowl. It was the size of a medium salad bowl, yet heavy. Molars and canine teeth had been set in the dark koa grain. The surface, inside and outside, was waxed, polished, smooth.

Next, the mask. He tried it on and looked at himself in the mirror. Focused on his eyes. His pupils large, black, fully dilated. *It fits well*, he thought, surprised. *Who else has worn this mask?* he wondered.

Liko gazed at the upright human form on the pedestal and wondered if it was a woman or a man, ancient or modern, Hawaiian or mainland. *Why is there a totem in Tamarind Park?* Clearly it lacked the fierceness necessary to protect the small green oasis of tamarind trees and manicured green grass and rectangular pools of cool water. He and Toi had arranged to meet at the small park in downtown Honolulu at the intersection of King and Bishop Street. He had arrived to discover the totem practically rising from a rectangular reflecting pool, surrounded by tall buildings. The small park bustled with harried office workers wearing aloha shirts, taking short lunch breaks, grabbing a quick smoke. Yeah, the sculpture was more inviting than protective. Maybe that was the point, he wondered. But it seemed to lack something. It seemed incomplete. How could something so passive protect the park from the tall buildings and the traffic? He concluded that it was probably a modern stone interpretation of a wooden Hawaiian tiki. But it seemed to lack something.

He waited five minutes, ten, fifteen. Finally his cell rang. It was Toi. She couldn't make it, a last-minute problem at work. And she had little time to talk. He groaned recalling that he was on summer vacation, while Toi and Keahi were working. Even the conversation would have to be short.

She said, "I know you're upset about the drowning. It's terrible."

"I know," he said.

"It's not your fault."

"I know that."

"I love you Liko. You're a wonderful person."

"You, too." Remembering their first date at the Waikiki Aquarium, he thanked her for sharing the monk seals with him, such amazing creatures. He also acknowledged that he was forever indebted to her for teaching him how to control his buoyancy in the mudflats.

And then he told her that he was returning to Nevada to finish his senior year. That precipitated a long silence.

Finally, Toi said she thought it best that he have the space during the coming year to 'discover himself' and 'to grow.' She said that he had been her best dive partner and that she would be looking forward to his next visit. But there was no passion, no sense of loss, no anxiety in her voice or words. Clearly she felt affection for him. But it was what she failed to say that upset him.

He read between the lines: she loved him, but she wasn't in love with him. She would miss him. She considered him a friend. A very special friend. She was hoping that their friendship would survive. But she wasn't in love. That choked him up.

"I'm so glad I met you," she said. "I never had a brother."

He reciprocated and called her 'sister,' though for him it felt like so much more. And since she couldn't see him, he allowed one and then two tears to flow down his cheeks.

After their goodbyes, as he watched the little phone symbol on his iPhone change from green to red, he wondered if he would ever be able to take another breath. He returned the phone to his front pants pocket.

He tried to wipe away his tears but they had already dried, evaporated. *Did they leave behind streaks of salt?* he wondered.

He looked around. No one seemed to have noticed him. He looked at the tiki again and decided he didn't like it. It was stupid.

After that the visit to Keahi's was easy. Liko walked the several miles to Keahi's studio, slowly. He was in no hurry. He wanted his sadness to pass before he arrived. Besides, his flight didn't leave for several hours.

It was hot and humid and he was covered in sweat when he arrived. Nevertheless, Keahi hugged him, kissed him on both cheeks, and wept when he heard that he was leaving later that evening.

Keahi offered him a Foster's on the lanai and he accepted. And then Keahi went inside to use the bathroom. He'd been drinking since getting off work and needed to relieve himself.

Waiting, Liko imagined that he was back at Hanauma Bay, scuba diving with Toi.

He inhaled and exhaled slowly, deeply three times. He unconsciously focused on the bright patches of light on the slate pool deck, then the bright sunlight reflecting on small blue pool tiles, and then on the light refracting off the surface of the pool as the wind gently stirred the water. All the while, he continued breathing deliberately, slowly, deeply. He felt the tension in his neck and rotated his head in an arch. He felt a vertebra pop. He focused next on all the blues: the blue in the sky, the blue shiny plastic strips stretched row-by-row across the back of the deck chairs, and the pale blue hydrangeas. Then the greens. And then the browns. He heard the wind rustling in the fishtail fronds overhead. And the far-off sound of an airplane departing. He could smell the faint odor of chloramines from the pool below. His own perspiration, his body salts. He smelled the moisture in the air. The smell of the ocean, sea salt. Gradually, a wonderful feeling of wholeness, oneness, filled him. "Narked," he said aloud, softly. He closed his eyes, took a long, exaggerated breath. And then he smiled. An uncontrollable smile. He opened his eyes wide. *I'm narked! And I'm not in the water.* He beamed with joy, delighted with his new discovery. It wasn't an oxygen-nitrogen imbalance relating to the depth of a dive.

ABOUT THE AUTHOR

Greg Olmsted is an environmental health specialist. He has Master of Science degrees in Environmental Health Science and Public Health. Olmsted hopes to use the arts to increase public awareness of environmental and public health issues. He resides with his wife in Washington, DC.